The Cat in the Hatbox

Charles Ray

North Potomac, MD

For information about this and other works of this author, contact the author at charlesray.author@yahoo.com.

Printed in the United States of America.

Cover photo by Kazuend

ISBN: 0692781609
ISBN-13: 978-0692781609

Dedication

To all the nice people I've met in retirement communities in the Washington, DC area. Your energy, enthusiasm, and sense of wonder have inspired me to create this series. I only hope I've done you proper justice.

.

One

Ed Lazenby lifted his fork. There was a sound like cardboard ripping. He stopped; his fork loaded with baked beans halfway to his mouth. He sniffed the air and made a face. The pungent smell stung his nose and made his eyes water.

"Jesus Christ, Ernie," he said. "If beans affect you that way, you should stop eating them, or bring Beano™ to every meal."

Ernesto Cardoza's face turned as red as a newly painted fire engine. He put the fork of beans he was about to shove into his mouth back down on the plate next to his hash brown potatoes. His cheeks puffed out, and he sighed.

"I forgot it this morning."

"Well, you shouldn't eat beans when you forget it," Ed said. He sniffed gingerly. The biting odor had abated, but still hung there, just under the smell of bacon and sausage wafting from the buffet line.

"Hey, there's nothing to worry about," Ernie said, frowning. "At least it wasn't the silent and deadly type."

Ed winced and looked around the room to see if any of the other diners had noticed his friend's loud explosion of gas. Fortunately, the table they occupied, not their usual one in the corner near the big window, but one near the entrance to the large dining room, wasn't near any occupied tables. Most of the elderly diners preferred tables near the large counter upon which the buffet meal was displayed, except for a couple of gentlemen who Ed recognized as the Ahearn brothers, who had gotten there first and taken table that he and Ernie usually occupied. He looked across the table and grimaced.

"It's still not polite, you know, but if the silent ones are worse than this, I guess I am ghankful."

"I can't help it. I tried holding it in, but you know how it is. It's gotta come out in one direction or the other, and I had a mouthful of food, so belching was out of the question."

"That, while not as smelly, would, I admit, have been just as bad," Ed said firmly, trying not to picture his friend spewing his food across the table. "I swear, Ernie, I can't take you anywhere without you doing something outrageous."

While putting his fork down, Ernesto cocked his head to the side and grinned at

Ed.

"Aw, come on, amigo, you know you like my company," he said. "If I didn't hang around with you, you'd have to put up with Violet and Rose, and you know how they can be."

Ed knew all right. Violet and Rose Wertheim were sisters who lived in a small, two-bedroom cottage at the southern end of Wisteria Street, at the opposite end from where Ed and Ernie's houses, similar two-bedroom cottages, sat across the street from each other. Violet, the eldest of the two, was domineering and opinionated, and never met anyone she couldn't find fault with, while Rose was shy and walked constantly in her sister's shadow, but the two of them were Ed and Ernie's best friends. Actually, Ed thought, they were about their *only* friends. The other residents of Potomac Valley Community, commonly called PVC after the material from which sewer pipes are made (and, in effect labeling their community as a dumping ground of sorts), were well south of 65, and given to sitting around in the evenings playing cribbage or talking about their grandchildren, while Violet and Rose, like Ed and Ernie, preferred a good game of five-card draw and a bottle of vodka along with conversation about something other than grandchildren, which none of them had. So, naturally, the four of them, when they felt like socializing, only had each other.

"I know Violet can be a bit trying," Ed said. "But, at least she doesn't stink up the room like you do."

"It's only when I eat beans or other high fiber food."

Ed made a growling sound deep in his throat and shoved the food he'd been holding into his mouth.

"Hey," Ernie said. "My reaction to beans is not what's bothering you."

Ed glared across the table. "Oh, what is it then?"

Ernie looked toward the corner table.

"You're pissed because Peter and Patrick took our table, and you're taking it out on me."

"Nah, that's not it." Ed shook his head, but he avoided making eye contact with his friend.

"Yeah? Well, if it's not, look me in the *eye* and say it, compadre."

Ed kept looking down at a wrinkle in the off-white tablecloth and played with the fork. "Uh, well . . ."

"Hah!" Ernie said. "I knew it. You can't look me in the eye."

Finally, Ed looked up, his brown face creased in a weak smile. "Okay, you got me. I was upset that the Ahearns got our table . . . but, what you did was still gross."

"Maybe, but if you'd confront them, or at least insist on joining them, you wouldn't be such a grouch."

Ed looked over at the two men. They were always dressed alike, even down to the way they combed their thinning white hair over the liver spots on their egg-shaped skulls, but didn't look quite the same age, although Ed suspected they might be twins. He'd only ever spoken to them once, two years earlier, right after moving to PVC; and it hadn't been a pleasant encounter. Patrick Ahearn, upon learning that Ed had just retired from his job as a systems analyst for the Department of Defense, made some comment about bloodthirsty warmonger, and then stared at Ed as if daring him to deny it. Peter stood next to his brother with a pugnacious stare on his face. Ed had been tempted to respond to Ahearn's taunt, but decided that it would only escalate into a senseless argument, so he ignored him, and that was the last time there had been any communication between them, albeit that time it was only one-way.

"Nah," he said. "Confrontation with assholes like that is a waste of energy, and I'd rather have breakfast with a skunk with poor bladder control than with those two. In fact, I guess I'd rather have breakfast with someone with a severe case of flatulence than sit with them."

Ernie looked confused. Ed had never shared the story of his only encounter with the Ahearns, which had taken place a couple of days before he and Ernie had met.

"Aw, come on, they can't be that bad. I

mean, you get along with Violet, and she's just about one of the meanest women on earth."

"Yeah, I know sometimes Violet can seem spiteful and hurtful," Ed said. "But, somehow, it's different." He described his encounter with the Ahearns. "When Violet insults you, it's personal, and right in your face. The way they did it, it was . . . different, like it had a meaning that I was missing."

Ernie shook his head. "I see your point. I never spoke to either of 'em, but I have to admit, they're a couple of strange ducks. I don't think anybody here at PVC gets along with 'em. But, I don't understand how you can get along with Violet and not with them."

Ed rubbed at his jaw, making a rasping sound that reminded him that he needed to shave.

"Well, I guess it's because Violet's insults are directly personal, you know, your socks don't match, or your breath smells; things you can ignore or laugh off; while they seemed to be going after something else entirely, like maybe insulting your beliefs, or something. Hell, I don't know, maybe they just piss me off." He paused and narrowed his eyes. "They remind me of a woman who was in the first section I was put in charge of at the Pentagon. The first day in charge, I discovered that she started every day at 8:00 sharp with a conference call."

"That doesn't sound like such a big

problem." Ernie looked puzzled.

"It was a *big* problem, my friend," Ed said. "She was a member of some evangelical sect, and that conference call, on government time and using a government phone system, was a prayer meeting she held with some of her co-believers around town. I told her as politely as I could that this was a misuse of government resources and that it had to stop immediately. Boy, was she ever pissed."

"Oh. What'd she do?"

"Nothing for the longest time; I thought she'd forgotten about it, until the following December when we were getting ready for the office holiday party. I used a marker pen and made a banner that said, 'Wishing everyone a Happy Xmas. When she saw it, she went ballistic. Went to HR and accused me of creating a hostile work environment. She didn't come right out and accuse me of sexual harassment, but when I talked to HR, it was clear that was the way they interpreted it. Back then, that was the kiss of death. I was lucky they didn't just give me my walking papers, but thankfully, the accuser was a bit on the fat side, and had a face that looked like a well-crumpled roadmap, so sexual harassment didn't make a lot of sense."

"Damn, what happened?"

Ed chuckled. "Nothing other than a lot of time wasted when I had to go and explain to the human resource officer what happened, and get one of my office mates who'd witnessed both incidents to make her statement.. When they bounced her complaint, she asked for a transfer, which was immediately and gladly approved. Turns out, I wasn't the first supervisor to get crosswise with her and get complained about."

Now, it was Ernie's eyes that screwed up in concentration. "Oh, yeah, I get it. It's one thing to insult your person, but something completely different when it's your beliefs."

"Right, so, no more talk about joining them. Let's finish our meal . . . that is, if your gas attack is done with."

"Okay, okay, no more beans."

Ed resumed eating, but he couldn't help but notice how his friend's eyes kept straying toward the still substantial pile of red beans on his plate.

"Oh, hell fire," he said. "Go ahead and eat the damn things. If you can't eat what you like when you get to be our age, what's the point?"

With a big smile on his brown face, Ernie began to quickly reduce the pile, taking his time to chew each mouthful carefully and slowly.

Ed chuckled as he finished the food on his plate. For a few minutes, they ate in relative calm—not absolute quiet, there were the clinking sounds of utensils against plates, and the occasional slurping sound of coffee being downed by someone who'd forgotten dentures and had to pull the liquid past gums. Then, the sound of bells shattered the calm.

The sound came from the far corner of the dining room, the area past the door to the kitchen which was, despite the large light fixtures hanging from the ceiling, always in shadow. No one really liked eating in the gloom, so there was only one table in the shadowy corner. Ed was surprised, therefore, to see the table occupied. A single diner sat with his back to the wall and a mobile phone at his ear.

Roland Vickers, MD, the CEO, director, and chief medical officer of Potomac Valley Community, sat alone at the table. That he was alone wasn't surprising; it seemed that no one sought the director's company if they could avoid it. But, it was the first time Ed had seen the man in the dining room.

Vickers was dressed as he usually was, a dark suit, white shirt and red tie, snug up against the prominent Adam's apple protruding from his scrawny neck. His thin lips were compressed in an expression of anger as he mumbled into the phone. He ran his free hand through the thin brown hair over his egg-shaped head, squinted at the phone, then slipped it into his pocket, stood and hurried through the dining room, ignoring the residents trying to get his attention as he passed their tables.

"I wonder what got him so excited," Ernie said.

"Probably his accountant calling to tell him profits are lower than estimated this quarter," Ed said. "Hey, hurry up and finish your food, we got a tee time in an hour."

There was another paper ripping sound from the vicinity of the rear of Ernie's pants. Ed rolled his eyes and threw his arms up in surrender. Ernie's cheeks turned red again, and.

"Geez, I stopped eatin' my beans. Whaddya want from me?"

"It's what I don't want from you that's really important. Please don't do that gas thing when I'm addressing the ball today."

"I promise you, you won't hear a thing," Ernie said.

Ed made a face and pinched his nose shut. "That's exactly what I'm afraid of. Don't do that either. If you just have to, walk away . . . far, far away."

Two

Breakfast was finished. Ed and Ernie, after stopping near the buffet table to ask Janet Murphy, PVC's head dietician, to thank the cook for a great meal, headed out, through the lobby, out through the double glass front doors of the reception area, and across the parking lot to the winding path that made its way between the two six-story condo buildings where it split, one fork going more or less southeast toward the golf course, and the other north toward Cypress Street, the main street that ran along the north side of PVC. Just before Cypress, the path forked again. Straight on it ran into Cypress, but they took the east-bound fork which paralleled Cypress until it came to Wisteria, ending beside Ed's two-bedroom bungalow, which sat facing Ernie's almost identical residence on the other side of the street.

Just as Ernie was about to cross the street to his house, a Montgomery Fire and

Rescue ambulance came careening around the corner from Cypress with the red lights flashing, causing him to jump back to the sidewalk. The ambulance whizzed by, south down Wisteria, and took a sharp right turn onto Maple, and was soon out of sight.

"I wonder what that's all about," Ernie said.

"Could be someone's sick," Ed said. "This is an old folks' home after all."

"Yeah, but I don't like that kind of reminder."

"I know what you mean. It kinda reminds me of one time when I worked at the Pentagon, they sent me to Tampa to work with the folks at MacDill Air Force Base. They put me up in a motel over the bay in St. Petersburg, where a lot of retirees live, and the sound of ambulance sirens kept me awake all night."

At the south end of Wisteria, they noticed people coming out of their houses and heading toward Maple. A small crowd had quickly formed, and, like the ambulance, it turned west on Maple and was soon out of sight.

"Think we should go take a look?" Ernie asked.

"Why don't we get our golf clubs? We have to go that way to get to the course. We can take a look before we tee off. It's probably nothing much."

"Yeah, you're probably right." Ernie

started across the street. "I'll meet you out here in a few minutes," he said over his shoulder as he took his key from his pocket and opened his front door.

Ed walked up and opened his own front door, and stepped into his sparsely, but neatly, furnished living room. He walked through the living room, past the tiny dining room and through the kitchen to the back patio where his golf bag and pull cart sat, just outside the kitchen door. He marveled that he could leave an expensive set of golf clubs outside, and find them when he returned. PVC, with its geriatric residents, was sometimes boring, but the crime rate was low. The only real crime it had ever had was the kidnapping of his friend Violet Wertheim by the golf course grounds keeper the previous year, a crime that Ed and Ernie had solved, even though they'd had to put themselves into a bit of danger in order to do it. Despite the lack of crime, though, he still checked to make sure his kitchen door was locked before grasping the handle of the pull cart and starting around toward the front of the house. 'Trust but verify,' was the slogan of a politician that he'd never liked very much, but the slogan made sense. Leaving his clubs outside on the days he planned to play golf was about as far as he was prepared to trust anyone. Not, mind you, that he had anything really worth stealing inside his house. His golf clubs and silver Toyota 4-

Runner were his most valuable possessions. He just believed that locks removed temptation, and kept honest people honest while making it harder for the crooks.

As he walked across the side yard, feeling the cushiony Bermuda grass beneath his feet, he looked up at the light blue canopy above him, with the sun, a white circle high up against the blue. He realized that he only ever really noticed the weather, or nature, when he was about to play golf. The rest of the time, it was just there, either good or bad—and, thunderstorms were the worst in his mind—but, not something you really noticed. It hadn't always been that way. When he was a young man, before he left home and joined the army, he'd liked nothing better than lying on his back in a field of clover, smelling the sweet aroma of honeysuckle and looking at the shapes of the clouds drifting against a blue sky. Somewhere along the way, perhaps his time in Vietnam, near the end of American involvement in late 1971 when a young Staff Sergeant Edward Lazenby had been assigned to 2d Battalion, 196th Infantry Brigade, one of the last American combat units left in Vietnam, he'd come to view the weather and nature as things to be wary of rather than enjoyed. On patrol in the jungle, rain masked the Viet Cong ambushes, and in clear weather, they just had better fields of fire. Forests and hills were ambush points, and small valleys just death traps. Now, over forty years later, he was only able to appreciate the weather and his natural surroundings when he played golf. He shook his head as he thought about that. Golf, the most frustrating pursuit known to man, and it turned out to be the thing that had helped him shake the devastating effects of post-traumatic stress disorder. No longer did stray sounds trigger images of orange and black gouts of flame or the crash of rocket propelled grenades. It had taken him nearly two decades to get past it, but for the past twenty years he'd been symptom free.

Ernie was waiting for him on the sidewalk in front of his house. Ed crossed the street to join him.

"You look like your mind's a million miles away," Ernie said.

"Oh, I was just thinking what a nice day it is."

Ernie looked up at the sky. "Yeah, it's a perfect day for golf; in fact, it's just a perfect day."

They started walking south, the wheels of their carts making creaking sounds that seemed to echo off the walls of the structures they passed. Just as they approached the intersection with Maple Street, Violet Wertheim, with her sister, Rose, approached them from the west. Both women wore ankle-length brown pants. Violet wore a bright blue short sleeved blouse, while Rose's was the same color as her pants. Violet, who was given to frequent hair color changes, had her close cropped hair died a reddish-brown color that was almost orange under the sunlight. Rose had allowed her white-streaked brown hair to grow out and had it done up in two buns on the sides over her ears. Violet walked with her back straight and her hands, fists clenched, at her side. She had what Ed realized was her 'put-upon' look on her face, her lips pressed together so tightly they were turning pale. Behind her, Rose, the shy sister, walked with her head down, clutching a round box to her chest.

"But, Violet," Rose said in a quiet voice that nonetheless carried up the street to Ed. "I couldn't just leave him there."

"The hell you couldn't have," Violet said without turning around to face her sister. "It's not our problem. You're always picking up strays."

"I couldn't just leave him there all alone."

"You damn well could have." Violet stopped and turned, wagging a finger in Rose's tear-streaked face. "Zelda was there. She could have taken care of him."

Rose began sobbing.

"Y-you know Zelda's schedule wouldn't permit her to p-properly take care of him."

"That's not my problem, now is it?"

"What's the problem ladies?" Ed asked. He and Ernie had turned right and were approaching the sisters. "What's in the box,

Rose?"

Violet threw her head back and looked down her long nose at him. "Please don't ask what's in the box," she said.

This, of course, only piqued Ed and Ernie's curiosity. They both stepped closer.

"C'mon, Rose," Ernie said, making his bushy black eyebrows bounce up and down. "Whatcha got in the box, huh?"

Rose stepped back, looking pleadingly at Violet.

"C-can I tell them, Violet?"

"Why ask me?" Violet looked as if she'd sniffed something noxious. "You didn't ask me when you picked that damn thing up, now did you?"

"I just couldn't leave him there all alone, that would have been cruel."

Ed stepped between the two women. He glared at Violet as he put a hand on Rose's shoulder.

"Now there, Rose," he said. "Why don't you tell us what's going on."

"Violet's upset because I took Petunia." Rose's lips quivered as she spoke, and more tears pooled in her eyes, threatening to join those that had already streaked the makeup on her slightly plump cheeks.

"Who's Petunia?" Ernie asked.

"Petunia's not a who," Rose said as she lifted the lid from the round box. "She's an it."

A round, furry face, white with light brown

markings on the head and cheeks, and large yellow eyes that were surrounded by the thick white fur, peered up at them. The large cat had been curled up, but when the lid was lifted, it sat up and took in its surroundings. Rose reached down and caressed its head, causing it to stretch its head up and make a 'br-r-r-r' sound.

"A cat . . . where the heck did you get a cat?" Ed asked.

"It belonged to Bea Terwilliger," Violet said, making another sniffing sound. "But now, thanks to my dimwitted little sister, I'll have to put up with having it around, shedding hair all over the place."

Ed vaguely recognized the name. Beatrice Terwilliger was an elderly widow in her late eighties, who had bought a cottage on Maple Street about six months earlier. He'd seen her a time or two in the dining room at the Community Center, but had never spoken to her.

"What happened? Did she decide taking care of a pet was too much for her?"

Violet and Rose shared a look. "Y-you don't know what happened, do you?" Rose asked.

"What happened?" Ed asked.

"Yeah, what happened?" Ernie echoed. "What kind of cat is that? Looks like a ball of yarn wrapped around a pair of eyes."

"It's a Persian," Rose said. "Well, mostly Persian, I think it has a mixed parentage. I never asked Bea. Do you know, Violet?"

"I don't know, and I don't *care*. I don't want a cat in my house."

"It's *our* house, Violet. I live there too."

Ed had never heard Rose stand up to her older sister before, but there she was, drawn up to her full five-two and staring back at the five-ten Violet with a tight jaw and rebellion in her eyes. Violet looked as shocked as Ed felt, but he doubted that she felt the pleasure he felt. He'd often wondered what it would take for Rose to rise up against her sister's bossiness—who would have thought it would have been a bundle of feline fur?

"So, why'd Beatrice Terwilliger give you her cat, Rose?"

"She didn't give it to her," Violet said. "Rose just took it."

"What!" Ed and Ernie said in unison.

"That's right, she just took it."

"Rose, you stole someone's cat?" Ernie asked.

"No, n-no, that's n-not the way it happened. I d-didn't steal Petunia." Her face was now slick with tears. "Oh, Violet, you tell them."

"Tell us what?" Ed turned to stare at Violet. "What the hell's going on here?"

"It's true, Ed, she didn't steal the damn cat," Violet said. "But, Bea was in no condition to give it to her. Besides, that woman would never give up Petunia. She was like a daughter to Bea."

"That's true," Rose said. "I don't think she cared as much for anyone as she does . . . did for Petunia."

Ed gave Ernie a pained look and got a shrug in return. "You just gotta let 'em tell the story their own way, amigo," Ernie said. "They'll get to the point eventually."

"Yeah, but I'd kinda like to get in eighteen holes at some point today."

"Oh, yeah, good point." Ernie pointed at Violet. "Come on, Violet, just tell us straight out how you guys got the cat so we can make our tee time."

"Oh, you men and your golf. I swear, I just do not understand what you see in it. You spend hours out there hitting that little ball around. It makes no sense."

Ed blew out a gust of air and made a growling sound.

"Then again," Ernie said. "I could be wrong about her getting to the point."

Normally a polite person, and almost— almost—accustomed to the way Violet had of ignoring the people around her, Ed was nonetheless becoming frustrated with her inability to focus. He'd asked what he thought was a simple question, one that could be easily answered, and she was meandering through that brain of hers, talking about anything but what he'd asked her. He turned away from Violet and looked down at Rose.

"Rose, can you *please* tell us how you got

the cat, so we can go play golf?" he asked.

Rose Wertheim looked like the scatterbrain in the family. With her wide eyes she looked perpetually surprised, and her soft voice and meek manner, people just assumed that she had little going on in her mind, and they just naturally deferred to Violet who had an opinion on everything, a steely glare that seemed to pin people to the wall, and a voice that carried across a large room. Ed knew better. He knew that behind Rose's mild mannered exterior there resided a first class mind and a big heart. It's just that she'd been in her big sister's shadow for so long, she seldom entered a conversation unless explicitly invited.

"I took the cat," she said. "Because Bea Terwilliger was just found dead in her house by her niece, Zelda, and Zelda's landlord doesn't allow pets, so I took Petunia to take care of because I know that's what Bea would have wanted."

Charles Ray

Three

Rose Wertheim didn't talk often and she didn't talk much, but on those rare occasions when she did, she more than made up for her periods of silence. The bombshell she dropped so unsettled Ed and Ernie that, after the two women agreed to join them that evening for a barbecue on Ernie's deck, and they went on to the golf course, the wheels came completely off their game. They played so badly, by the tenth hole they'd stopped keeping score, and by number fourteen, they quit in disgust and stormed off the course, much to the delight of a foursome behind them who either hadn't heard of the death in the community, or were so immersed in the game that they'd blocked it out.

Ed was still mulling it over in his mind at 6:00 that evening as he crossed the street to Ernie's house. He found his friend on his back patio, stacking charcoal briquettes on a large grill. Two plastic trays covered with aluminum foil sat on the picnic table at the edge of the patio. Ed put the case of Heineken beer he carried on the table next to the trays.

"Ice chest's under the table," Ernie said. "Whyn't you put a few cans in to get cool."

"They're already cool. I had them in the fridge. Want one?"

"I wouldn't say no."

Ed pulled the case open and extracted two cans. He opened one and handed it to Ernie and the other for himself. After putting his beer on the table, he took ten cans out of the case and, kneeling, put them into the red Styrofoam ice chest under the table, wiggling and jamming them down into the ice before putting the top back on the chest. Ed popped the tab on the can and took a long pull. After lowering the can, he wiped his lips and sighed. He looked at Ernie who was staring down at the orange flames licking at the lumps of charcoal. He had a sad look on his face.

"Why are you looking so down, bro?" he asked.

"Oh, I was just thinking about how tenuous life is. We're here one day and gone the next."

"You get all that from staring at burning charcoal?"

"No, man, I was thinking about Beatrice Terwilliger dying."

"Hey, people die, especially old people."

"Yeah, I know, but when it's someone you know it just kind of . . . hits home, you know."

"But, you hardly knew her, I don't think anyone here really knew her," Ed said. "She hardly ever came to the community center. I mean, I'm not sure I ever even spoke to her."

The flames died down, leaving the charcoal coated in white with smoke drifting up in lazy spirals. Ernie turned and began lifting the foil from one of the trays, revealing several small flank steaks. He began arranging them on the iron grill.

"You know what I mean, Ed," he said. "We might not have been close to her, but we *knew* her. Well, maybe we didn't exactly know her, but she was part of the community."

Ed did know what he meant, but he'd forced it from his mind almost as soon as he'd been told. It was something he'd long ago learned to do.

In January 1972, Ed was in his second year in the army. He'd missed out on being sent to Vietnam up to that time, had made corporal, and was looking forward to being sent to the Infantry School at Fort Benning, Georgia as a junior instructor, without ever having experienced combat. He was surprised, though, when his battalion sergeant major called him to headquarters and informed him that his transfer to

Benning had been cancelled, and he, along with several other young noncommissioned officers, would report for duty with the 196th Infantry Brigade in Vietnam. President Nixon's Vietnamization program was set to be implemented the following year, but the peace talks in Paris were floundering, so it was decided that the 196th, one of few American units left in country, needed some fresh blood to provide security for the few bases left.

Ed arrived at Tan Son Nhut Airbase in late February, and was immediately assigned to 2d Battalion's Quick Reaction Force, a platoon of 40 riflemen led by a second lieutenant who was his first tour, having only been commissioned six months before arriving in country. The QRF, as it was called, was always on standby, but after the peace talks broke down in March, and the North Vietnamese launched their 1972 Easter Offensive, standby duty quickly became being airlifted from one fire fight to another. That was the first time Ed had seen death up close and personal. Two of the corporals who had come with him from his old unit were killed during the first four months. By the time the 196th was pulled out of Vietnam in August, he'd seen twelve of the men in the QRF transported away in body bags, and had learned to mourn silently while keeping his weapon at the ready and doing his job. He remembered each man, but after the first two hadn't shed a tear for the rest. He just felt survivor's guilt, a normal reaction in those who come out of a battle alive while men around them are cut down. It was neither a good nor bad feeling—more like a hollow in the center of your chest and a pull at your emotions, one part of you wanting to jump and shout because you were still alive, and another part feeling ashamed that you *were* still alive. It was pretty damned uncomfortable. It was what he was feeling at that moment. Not sadness, not happiness, just a nagging discomfort, like the feeling you get when you get a crease in the bottom of your socks and you're in no place where you can take your shoes off and smooth it out.

So, while he understood Ernie's feelings, he couldn't share them. Death, he knew, comes to all eventually. It was just Beatrice Terwilliger's time. But, he also knew that Ernie, who had escaped military service because of flat feet—which, however, hadn't disqualified him from walking a postman's route for decades—had caused the army to refuse him when he tried to enlist, wouldn't, couldn't understand his reaction, so he did what he always did, he felt bad. It wasn't a faked feeling. He could tell that from the look in his friend's eyes.

"Yeah, it's always sad when someone in the community dies," he said. "But, she lived a good long life, and hopefully, her end was peaceful."

Ernie took a long pull from his beer and then took a large fork and turned the steaks. "Yeah, there is that. Say, you want your steak medium rare as usual?"

"Brown on the outside, pink on the inside," Ed replied. "You know how I like it."

"Like what?" a raspy voice asked.

Both men turned to see Violet Wertheim coming around the corner of the house carrying a large bowl covered with plastic wrap. She was followed closely by Rose who still carried the hatbox clutched to her chest.

"Evening ladies," Ed said. "I was describing how I like my steak cooked."

"Of course, that's also how I bet he likes a few other things," Ernie said.

Violet sniffed. "Ernesto Cardoza, your mind's always in the gutter."

Rose giggled.

Ernie ignored Violet's comment, focusing his attention on Rose. "Rose, my dear, how would you like your steak cooked?"

"Well done, please."

"Aren't you going to ask me how I want mine?" Violet put the bowl on the table and faced him with her hands on her hips and her chin jutted out.

"Don't have to," he said. "You want your steak to match your personality, dry, dark and crusty."

Rose giggled again, and Ed quickly lifted his beer to his lips to stifle a laugh, making a barking, gurgling sound instead. Violet's head whipped around, staring, first at Rose and then at Ed. "You find that funny, Ed Lazenby?"

He lowered the can and wiped the foam from his lips. "Why no, Violet, not at all," he said. "I just drank my beer too fast and almost choked."

She continued to pin him with a steely glare that made him feel uneasy. He didn't want to spoil the evening by starting an argument with Violet.

"Say, Rose, is that the box the cat was in?" Ed asked, drawing everyone's attention away from Ed. "Did you bring the cat with you?"

Rose's cheeks darkened and she looked down at the box that she still held tightly to her chest. "Uh, yes; I hope you don't mind."

"I told you that mangy animal should have been left at home," Violet said. Her attention was now firmly on her sister.

"B-but, he was crying when it looked like we were leaving him alone. I j-just couldn't." Rose looked at Ernie; a pleading look in her eyes.

"Aw, that's no problem," Ernie said. "He can eat the leftovers."

"Petunia's a female," Rose said.

"Oh, I mean *she* can eat the leftovers."

"Just keep her away from *my* food," Violet said. She turned back to face Ernie. "How long will it be until the food's ready?"

"Not long, not long. Just keep your shirt on. Why don't you two have a cold beer while the meat finishes cooking?"

Rose put the box on the table, too near the covered bowl for Ed's comfort, and knelt to get beers from the cooler. She handed one to Violet, who sniffed disdainfully, but took it. After opening it and taking a sip, she put it on the table and picked the box up again.

"Poor cat must be pretty tired of being cooped up in that hatbox," Ed said.

"I'm sure she is," Rose said. "But, I wasn't sure it would be a good idea to let her out around strangers."

"You're not worried she'll run away, are you?"

"No, I took her into our backyard, and she stayed right at my side."

Ernie flipped a couple of steaks. Fat dripping off the meat hit the smoldering charcoal, sizzling loudly and giving off the heady aroma of hickory and beef, making Ed's mouth water. The box in Rose's hands jiggled and a muffled 'meo-o-o-ow' came from within.

"Sounds like she wants to be outside," Ed said.

Gingerly, Rose removed the lid from the hatbox. A furry, round head, covered in white fur, slowly emerged. Unblinking, the cat looked around, fixing each of the humans with an icy stare. Rose put the hatbox on the patio and stepped back.

Slowly, two furry white paws appeared on the rim of the box. The cat rose up on its hind legs, its bushy tail waving sinuously from side to side.

"Come on, Petunia," Rose said. "You can come out and play." She squatted and held a hand out, palm up, wiggling her fingers.

Petunia fixed its wary eyes on Rose's fingers. Then, she vaulted over the rim of the box, and ran to Rose, rubbing her side against Rose's hand and purring softly.

Rose looked up at Ed. She smiled a broad smile that lit up her eyes. "See, didn't I tell you she was friendly?"

After a few minutes, Petunia drew back from Rose's hand and turned. Her round head swiveled as she looked, first at Ed and then at Ernie. She raised her head and sniffed daintily, and then walked over and began rubbing against Ernie's legs.

"Well, I guess we know who has the most drawing power as far as the ladies are concerned," Ernie said.

"Or who has the smell of fresh meat all over him," Ed shot back.

"If that's what it takes, you're not gonna hear me complain." He picked up a knife from the rack attached to the side of the grill and cut a tiny sliver of meat off one of the steaks. After blowing on it for a few minutes, he knelt and offered it to Petunia.

She sniffed at it, and then opened her mouth and gently took it from him, chewing quickly and swallowing, and then licking her muzzle with her long pink tongue. She then sat and looked up at Ernie, making a mewing sound.

"Yeah, but you have to keep feeding her to keep her attention," Ed said.

"No, no more for now, kitty," Ernie said. "You can have more when we all eat."

Petunia's head cocked to one side as she peered up at Ernie. Then, with a haughty toss of her head, she stood and walked to Ed and began rubbing against his leg. Not exactly a cat person, Ed was unsure of what to do, so he simply leaned over and ran his fingers lightly over her back. She arched up against his fingers and made purring noises.

"She likes you, Ed," Rose said. "And, you don't have to feed her to get her to do it." She grinned mischievously at Ernie as she spoke.

Unmindful of the verbal interplay among the humans, Petunia rubbed against Ed's leg one last time and then walked over to where Violet was sitting and, standing squarely in her line of sight, looked up at her and purred louder. Violet frowned down at her, but didn't otherwise move or acknowledge her.

After a thirty-second staring contest, Petunia stepped forward until her head was nearly touching Violet's shin. She looked up and purred again, a sound like a night bird. When Violet still didn't move, Petunia eased up closer and began twining her body between Violet's legs, purring as she snaked across the shin of her left leg and the calf of the right. When she'd made it completely through, she rubbed her body up and down against Violet's right leg.

After a few seconds of this, Violet's hand dropped down beside her leg and she buried the tips of her fingers in the thick hair of Petunia's back. Petunia arched her back and purred even louder.

"Well, I'll be damned," Ed said. "She even likes you, Violet."

Violet tried glaring at him, but her mouth didn't quite make it to a full frown. "What's not to like? This cat's just a good judge of character."

Charles Ray

Four

Ed woke up early Saturday morning, planning to fix a big breakfast and then do some work with the flowers around the base of the house. As he walked through the living room, heading for the kitchen, he noticed the corner of a flyer under his front door. He picked it up and saw that Roland Vickers was inviting all the residents of PVC to a special brunch meeting in the dining room of the community center at 10:00. It was marked IMPORTANT!! in red ink as if the all-caps and exclamation point didn't sufficiently convey the message, so he decided he would just eat toast and coffee and save his appetite for the brunch.

Two slices of dry toast and a cup of instant coffee later, he was dressed in a pair of faded jeans and a tattered white tee shirt, on his knees at the north side of his house pulling dandelions from among the ferns he'd planted there to take advantage of the almost permanent shade on that side of the structure. Damn dandelions seemed to thrive anywhere, snapping back after being zapped with weed killer—not that he'd ever use it for fear of killing the other plants or harming the wildlife that hung out in the ferns. They even regrew after he mowed, within days in fact. The only thing that seemed to reduce their numbers—temporarily—was pulling them out by the roots and dumping them on the curb for the recycling truck that came every Tuesday morning. At least the ferns were lush and green. They didn't seem to mind sharing space with the noxious weeds.

After getting all the dandelions he could see on the north side, he dumped them into a dark green plastic bag and moved to the front yard. When he saw the number of the colorful, but noxious, weeds on his tiny front lawn, he shrugged and sighed.

"Darn," he said to himself, dropping the bag on the ground. "It'll take hours to even make a dent in all this."

"Why don't you just buy weed killer?" Ed hadn't noticed Ernie crossing the street. "That's what I do, and you can see, my lawn's dandelion free."

"I hate spraying poisons around willy nilly," Ed said. "It kills more than just the weeds, you know. What about the birds who feed on the insects in the grass?"

Ernie's brows wiggled and he frowned. "You're not gonna guilt me into crawling 'round on my hands and knees pullin' weeds, amigo, so just forget it."

Ed looked around at his yard. The grass was a nice deep green, he thought. And, the little yellow dots were scattered pretty much evenly across the whole expanse of the yard. Not a bad look when you stop and think about it.

"That's exactly what I plan to do," he said. "You want to join me for a cup of coffee to kill time until we go for this brunch Vickers is inviting us to?"

"Sure, why not? I wonder what's so important he has to call a special last minute brunch?"

Ed just shrugged. With PVC's CEO one could never tell. Ernie followed him around back and into the kitchen. He busied himself at the kitchen counter, preparing coffee, freshly ground instead of instant, while Ernie plopped himself down at the small table in the breakfast nook.

When the coffee pot began burbling, Ed joined his friend at the table. The two men sat in silence, enjoying the aroma of coffee that was quickly filling the room. True friends that they were, conversation was unnecessary in moments like this. They were able to enjoy each other's company without the need to fill the silence. It reminded Ed of the camaraderie he'd enjoyed with the men in his platoon in Vietnam. Between patrols, if they weren't in the tent that served as the enlisted club drinking beer, or in someone's hooch playing cards, they'd just lounge around on the sandbags staring up at the sky, not talking, just enjoying being alive, and, for those few moments, not being shot at.

When the sounds of the coffee pot stopped, Ed rose and filled two white ceramic mugs and returned to the table. He blew on his and watched as Ernie dumped two teaspoons of sugar into his, blew on it and took a long sip.

They took their time sipping coffee, with Ed occasionally glancing at the clock over the counter. At 9:15, he drained the rest of his coffee and took the empty mug to the sink. Ernie noisily finished his and put his mug into the sink next to Ed's. Ed rinsed out both mugs and put them upside down on the corrugated drain pad next to the sink. He headed for the door. He didn't bother telling Ernie why he was leaving the house so early, because he figured he would already know; he wasn't about to let the Ahearns get his favorite table yet again.

Not many people were heading to the community center as early as they were; mostly those who needed walkers or canes who, if they didn't go early, would be late and have to take the worse tables. Ed recognized a few, nodding at them as he and Ernie walked past.

They arrived at the community center at 9:20. There were only a few tables occupied in the dining room. Violet sat at their favorite table, staring up at the Ahearn twins who stood on either side of her, glaring down at her.

"You can't just take a whole table for yourself," Ed heard Patrick Ahearn say as he and Ernie neared the table.

"I told you," Violet said. "I'm saving places for some friends who will be here any moment now."

"I don't believe you," Peter said from her right side. He balled his fists up and hunched forward.

"You wouldn't be thinking of hitting a lady, now would you, Peter?" Ed asked.

He walked around the table and placed himself between Violet and Peter Ahearn. Ernie walked around the other side and stood near Patrick with a menacing look on his face.

"Everything okay, Violet?" Ernie asked.

"Everything's fine," she said. "The Bobbsey Twins here were insisting that this was *their* table even though I got here first."

Ed fixed Peter with a glacial look. "How interesting. Ernie and I have been sitting at this table for more than two years, long before the two of you moved here. How did it become your table all of a sudden?"

Peter's face screwed up in an expression of confusion. He looked at his brother.

"It's first come, first served," Patrick said. "We get here before you do, so it's our table, not yours."

Ed made no effort to hide the smile that came. The Ahearns looked puzzled as he began to chuckle.

"You know," he said. "I never cease to be amazed at how thickheaded bullies are. You just shot the shit out of your own argument, and you're so full of yourself you didn't even realize what you were doing."

"W-whaddaya mean?" the brothers asked in unison.

"If it's first come, first served, dunderhead, then the table is mine, since I got here before any of you," Violet said.

Ed's smile got broader. "What she said."

Patrick Ahearn was the first to realize that they'd been beaten, and by their own words. His shoulders sagged. A few seconds behind his brother, Peter looked like a dog had just peed on his pants leg.

"Oh," they both said.

Ernie stepped around to stand behind Violet. "Now, beat it boys."

"We don't have to leave," Peter said. "You can't make us."

Violet stood up, and at an inch taller than the brothers, loomed over them. "I bet you that if I kicked you little baboons in the balls you'd leave," she said.

Peter backed up, while Patrick covered his groin with his hands. "Y-you wouldn't d-dare," Patrick said.

She balled up a bony fist and raised it.

The Brothers Ahearn paled and shrank back from her even though she hadn't raised her fist at either one in particular. Peter brushed against Ed as he scooted past him, but Patrick, upon looking up into Ernie's glowering face, opted for brushing first the window and then the wall as he made his getaway. Violet laughed as the Ahearns scampered across the room, finally settling for a table in the farthest corner from Ed's favorite window, both sitting with their backs to Ed, Ernie and violet.

"Well, I guess that'll show them," Violet said.

"Where's Rose?" Ernie asked.

Violet was still chuckling as she sat back down. "Oh, Petunia's having separation issues," she said. "She kicked up such a fuss when we started out the door we decided that one of us should stay with her at all times for a while until she settles down."

Ed was surprised that Violet was referring to the animal by name instead of 'that damned cat,' but he kept his expression neutral as he sat across from Violet. It looked like she was becoming attached to Petunia. Of course, even though he himself wasn't a cat person, he could see how that could happen. Petunia looked like a dust mop with ears with her fluffy white fur going off in all directions. And, she had the most pleasant disposition Ed had ever seen in a feline.

"Well, we can get Janet to fix her a plate of

something nice," he said. "She's probably the lucky one. She won't have to listen to Vickers natter on."

"Speak of the devil," Ernie muttered.

Roland Vickers, wearing a pearl gray suit, beige shirt and bright green tie, strode through the entrance to the dining room.

Just inside the door, Vickers paused and looked around. He fiddled with his tie, which didn't really need straightening, and flicked at imaginary specks of dust on the sleeves of his jacket. Then, he began his stately march across the room toward the center where Ed noticed Janet Murphy stood beside a pole microphone. Vickers nodded at people as he passed their tables, but didn't stop to speak with anyone. He was playing the part of royal potentate to the hilt.

When he reached Murphy, she tapped on the microphone, the 'thump, thump' of her fingers echoing off the walls. "Ladies and gentlemen," she said, her voice sounding tinny coming from the speakers mounted in the four corners of the room. "May I have your attention please? I'd like to introduce our director, Dr. Roland Vickers." Conversations ceased. The only sounds were a few people coughing—to be expected in a roomful of people of advanced years and uncertain health—and a few cups made tinkling sounds as they were placed on saucers. "Thank you," Murphy continued. "Dr. Vickers, the floor is yours."

She stepped aside, and Vickers stepped up. Despite her having just successfully tested it, he tapped on the mike, and then cleared his throat. There was a squawk of feedback as he leaned in with his mouth too close to the surface. His eyes widened and he pulled his head back, looking like someone who's been stung by a bee after sniffing at a flower. Quickly, though, he regained his composure and cleared his throat again.

"Good morning, Potomac Valley Community residents," he said. "I'm honored to be here with you this morning." He paused and looked at Murphy, his brow wrinkling. She handed him a glass of water. He took a sip. After wiping his lips daintily, he looked around at the sea of wizened faces. "I only wish that our gathering this morning was for a happier purpose."

"This guy takes longer to get to the point than an unsharpened pencil," Ernie whispered to Ed.

"He just likes to hear himself talk," Violet said. She didn't whisper, and the old couple at the table next to theirs looked at her and smiled nervously.

"Please, Violet, your voice carries even when you try to whisper," Ed said.

"I wasn't trying to whisper."

The old couple looked at each other and giggled, which attracted Vickers' attention.

"It's really nothing to laugh about," he said, shooting a withering glare at them. "I have the sad duty to announce the passing of one of our residents. Some of you probably knew her; Beatrice Terwilliger; she passed away yesterday morning. I would like to ask that we all observe a moment of silence to her memory."

He bowed his head and put his right hand over his the left breast pocket of his jacket, discretely adjusting the handkerchief in it.

For thirty seconds the only sound was the shuffle of shoes against the floor. Then, Vickers dropped his hand to his side and again glanced around the room. He tried to look solemn, but to Ed it looked like he was either constipated or had a bad case of gas.

"We will be holding a memorial service for Beatrice a week from tomorrow at the community chapel."

A stoop-shouldered man with white, wispy hair that stuck out from his round head in all directions, who was seated at the table directly in front of where Vickers stood, raised a gnarled hand.

"Yes, Mr. . . . Collins? You have something to say?" Vickers asked, looking put upon that someone would have the nerve to horn in on his moment at center stage.

Collins, his nose red and bulbous, and crisscrossed with a network of darker red veins, looked like a garden gnome. When he spoke, his squeaky voice added to the impression that someone had worked a magic spell to bring a garden ornament to life.

"What'd she die from?" he asked.

Vickers cleared his throat. "It was a heart attack," he said.

"Did she suffer much?" Collins asked.

Ed clenched his jaw, grinding his molars together. No matter how long he lived in PVC, he could never get used to the morbid fascination some of its residents had with death and suffering. Out of the corner of his eye he saw that Violet's brow was wrinkled and her lips were turned down in a scowl.

"I doubt it," Vickers said. "I think the end came quickly and she passed peacefully."

Violet made a snorting sound.

"I think I agree with you," Ed whispered. "I can't imagine a heart attack being a peaceful way to go either. Hell, the only way I'd be willing to call death peaceful is if it came when I was sleeping, and I didn't know it was happening."

Violet leaned forward, still frowning. "Especially when it *wasn't* a heart attack," she said. This time, she did whisper.

"What do you mean, it wasn't a heart attack? You heard what Vickers just said, and he's a doctor, he should know what he's talking about."

"I was there, Rose and me, when they took her away," she said, still whispering. "I saw her face just before they zipped the bag shut. She didn't look like she went peacefully. And, we talked to Zelda, her niece . . . she's the one who found her . . . and, from what she said, I don't think Beatrice had a heart attack."

Ed knew Violet Wertheim to be a contrary personality, and there was certainly no love lost between her and PVC's CEO, especially after her little kidnapping stunt had forced him to pony up funds to hire a chef for the dining room. But, there was something in the tone of her voice and the glint in her eyes that made Ed pay attention.

"What makes you think that?" he asked.

She leaned back in her chair. "Zelda's coming to our house tomorrow morning. We're helping her make the final arrangements. Why don't we come to your house, and I'll let her explain it to you."

Five

The rest of Ed's Saturday crept by like cold molasses from a narrow-necked bottle. He couldn't get Violet's words out of his mind. Normally, he paid little attention to her ranting and ruminations, but she'd seemed so sure of herself, he couldn't help but wonder if perhaps there wasn't something to what she said. It hadn't surprised him when Violet disagreed with Vickers; hardly anyone that Ed knew in PVC really liked the man with his officious, patronizing ways. But, she'd expressed support for someone else's opinion at the same time, and that was something he didn't remember ever seeing her do. He didn't know Beatrice Terwilliger's niece; he didn't really know Beatrice; but he couldn't imagine her being the type Violet would be sympathetic with. Violet wasn't even sympathetic with her own baby sister.

No, Ed thought, there's more here than meets the eye. What we have here is a puzzle, one that needs to be solved. Actually, to Ed, every puzzle needed to be solved.

When he woke up Sunday morning, it was still on his mind. It was on his mind as he ate a breakfast of Cheerios with fresh strawberries and instant coffee, having decided to try and talk Ernie into having a late brunch—or early lunch—with him at the community center. Maybe he'd be able to pick up some gossip there. Then he remembered that Violet said that Zelda was coming to visit the morning. So, he decided as he spooned Cheerios into his mouth, maybe it might be a good idea to take everyone to brunch. That way I can get Zelda's views, and get several points of view all at the same time. He smiled at his hazy reflection in the refrigerator door—that's the efficient way to solve a puzzle.

Just like Violet, he thought as he sat in his living room with the Sunday *Washington Post* spread out in front of him with a second cup of coffee next to it, not to give a specific time for Zelda's arrival, forcing everyone to rearrange their schedules around her. He'd called Ernie and given him a head's up, now he had to kill time until Violet called to let him know that Zelda had arrived and they were on their way to the community center.

He was midway through solving the puzzle in the back of the *Sunday Post* magazine insert when his doorbell rang. He put the magazine on the coffee table and went to the door, opening it to Ernie who stood grinning on his front step.

"Hey, amigo," Ernie said. "Thought I'd drop over and have coffee with you. Whatcha doing?"

Ed stepped aside and let his friend enter. "Just working the Sunday crossword puzzle." He looked at his watch. It was 9:45. "Violet said Beatrice's niece was coming this morning, but I haven't heard from her yet. I thought when she called I'd suggest we all go to the community center for Sunday brunch." So, you got bored sitting around waiting, and decided to come over and bug me, Ed thought. Ed knew his friend well. Ernie was as anxious to get started working on this puzzle as Ed was, but he wasn't the type who did very well sitting by himself with nothing to do. No, he'd much rather sit quietly in a room with Ed with nothing to do. In truth, Ed didn't mind. "I'm just having instant coffee, by the way, but you're welcome to join me."

Ernie walked to the sofa and picked up the magazine, wrinkling his brow as he looked at the puzzle.

"You're only half finished. You want I should brew a pot of coffee while you work on it?"

"Okay. You know where everything is. Check the top shelf of the pantry; I just bought some fresh Jamaican beans last week. The coffee grinder's up there too."

Ernie disappeared into the kitchen. Ed sat on the sofa and resumed working on the puzzle. He was down to the next to last across clue when the phone rang.

"Ed Lazenby here," he said after he picked it up.

"Ed, this is Violet. Zelda Terwilliger just arrived; can we come to your place?"

"Sure, but I was thinking we could all meet at the community center for brunch."

There was a long few seconds of silence.

Finally, Violet spoke, "Uh, Zelda would rather talk in private. Could we just do sandwiches at your place?"

Fortunately, he'd done a grocery run when he bought the new coffee beans, so his pantry and fridge held enough to deal with the extra mouths.

"Sure," he said. "What time can you come over?"

"We can be there by 10:30. Is that okay?"

Like he really had a choice. His curiosity was aroused; he had to find out what was going on. "Sure, that's fine," he said.

Violet, true to form, broke the connection without acknowledging his agreement. In fact, he heard the click of the broken connection before he'd finished speaking. She'd heard him say 'sure,' and that was enough for her. Shrugging, he put the phone down and stood.

When he walked into the kitchen, he

found Ernie standing at the counter watching the dark brown coffee drip into the clear glass pot.

"Hope you made a full pot," Ed said. "We have company coming."

"Violet, Rose, and Beatrice's niece, right?"

"Yeah, they don't want to eat at the community center. I was thinking sandwiches and salads would be nice."

"When do they get here?"

Ed looked at his watch. "Ten minutes," he said. "What can we prepare in that time?"

"You got any tuna fish?"

"Sure, I just recently restocked my pantry." He snapped his fingers. "Right! We can do tuna salad, that's even quicker than sandwiches. You toast some bread and I'll fix the salad."

Ernie removed a loaf of bread from the freezer and began the process of toasting the frozen slices, while Ed took three large cans of tuna from the pantry. Five minutes later, they stepped back and admired their handiwork; Ernie had a stack of golden brown toast slices smeared with butter and a sprinkling of garlic powder on a plate, and Ed had a bowl of tuna, diced tomatoes, chopped green onions and jalapeno peppers mixed with mayonnaise and spicy yellow mustard sitting on the counter.

"Now, that's what I call a quick lunch," Ernie said, raising his right hand for a high five, which Ed returned.

"Let's get the table set. They'll be here any minute."

They'd just finished setting five places at Ed's dining table when the chime of his doorbell echoed through the house.

Ed rushed into the living room and opened the door.

Violet, a large bowl in her arms, stood in front of his door. She wasn't smiling, not exactly, but the strained look of someone with a bad case of constipation was what Ed recognized as her attempt at the unfamiliar facial expression. Behind her and to her right stood Rose, clutching the hatbox from which could be heard a loud, but contented-sounding purring. To Rose's left stood a young woman, he assumed it was Zelda Terwilliger, of medium height who immediately caught Ed's eye. It was no one single thing that captured his attention as he eyed her from head to toe and back; but, a combination of things. First, she had dark makeup encircling her bright blue eyes, blue-black lipstick covering thick, pouty lips, short, spiked hair colored in stripes of red, green, and blue that stood up and out from her head. She wore a sleeveless, faded denim shirt, exposing the intricate tattoos of snakes and roses on both fairly well-muscled for a woman arms. The tattoos ran from her shoulders to her wrists. She had her hands planted on her hips, and as Ed looked, it took an effort not to gape openly. She had slightly broad shoulders and strong arms, practically no breasts pushing out the denim shirt, but her hips flared out to the sides like a pair of clown pants. Ed figured you could balance a shot glass on either side. He let his eyes keep moving downward where he saw that she wore a pair of pink flip-flop sandals, revealing tiny feet with long toes, the nails painted purple. Ed took a breath.

"Violet, Rose, you're right on time," he said, stepping aside. "Come on in. Ernie and I just finished making tuna salad and toast."

The three women squeezed past. He caught a whiff of a flowery scent as Zelda passed him.

"I brought potato salad," Violet said. "Maybe we can make toasted tuna sandwiches to go with it."

"Makes sense. Let's go into the dining room. Rose, I assume that's Petunia you have in the box."

"Yes," Rose said. "She's still fussy about being left alone."

"Can't say I blame her," the young woman said. She had a deep, melodious voice.

"Oh, by the way, Ed, this is Zelda, Beatrice's niece," Violet said. "Zelda, this is Ed Lazenby, he's our resident Sam Spade."

Zelda looked confused. "Sam who?"

"Sam Spade was a private eye created by Dashiell Hammett in the 1930s," Ed said. "And, it is in no way a description of me."

"No," Rose said. "Ed's more of a Miss

Marple."

Now, Zelda looked even more confused.

"A slightly more contemporary character," Ed said. "From Agatha Christie, who you probably don't recognize any more than you recognize Dashiell Hammett."

"You think? You guys are like as freaky as my . . . Aunt Bea." Her eyes glistened with unshed tears. She shook her head and made her way to the couch where she plopped down and put her head in her hands.

Rose walked over and put the hatbox on the floor near her feet, sat and put her arm around her shoulders.

"There, there now, honey," she said. "We know you miss your aunt. We all do. But, Dr. Vickers said she went peacefully."

The top on the hatbox bounced twice and then popped off. Petunia's fluffy head emerged from the box's innards and swiveled around, taking in the entire room before coming to rest oriented in Zelda's direction. With a 'yowl,' Petunia vaulted out of the box and jumped into Zelda's lap, nuzzling her head against Zelda's tiny breasts and purring contentedly.

"Petunia, baby," Zelda said as she ran her fingers through the cat's hair. "How you been? You miss me?" Petunia purred louder, and flipped over onto her back to allow Zelda to tickle her tummy. "I missed you too. Who's a nice girl, eh?"

"She really seems to like you," Ed said.

Zelda looked up at him, smiling wanly. "Aw, Petunia likes everybody. She's like a little baby, hates to be ignored, and is always sticking her nose into things. Aunt Bea treated her like a child."

"I know about the 'hate to be ignored' part," Rose said. "Every time we leave the house, she kicks up such a fuss if we don't take her with us."

"Oh? That's new. That must be from like being locked in the closet."

"What do you mean by that?" Ed asked.

Zelda's face clouded over. "When I . . . found my aunt . . . Petunia was locked in the front closet. Poor baby was crying and scared to death. She must have been like trapped in there accidentally before Aunt Bea . . ."

"You said *locked* in the closet. Was the door just closed, or was it locked?"

"Oh, no, it was locked," she said. "I remember having to like turn that little gizmo to get it to open."

Ed thought on that. He didn't know what it signified, but it was a clue. No, he thought, I'm not getting involved in this. His interior monologue—sort of an argument with himself—went like this:

Ed: I'm not one to judge people, but this girl's a strange one; all those tattoos on her arms, and that weird hair. I'll bet she even uses drugs. So many young people today do.

Ed's alter ego: Now, now, don't be so quick to condemn based on external appearances.

Deep inside she's probably a nice person. The cat likes her.

Ed: True. She seemed a little aggressive when she first came in, her hands on her hips and all, but she just lost her aunt, so I should be prepared to make some allowances. And, I mustn't forget, there's a mystery to be solved here.

Ed's alter ego: Is that all it is to you, just a mystery?

Ed: Well, I do like to help people in need, but let's face it; I simply cannot resist an unsolved puzzle.

Ed's alter ego: Whatever.

Ed: Something's afoot, and I've just got to find out what it is.

He smiled at Zelda, studiously avoiding looking at her arms or her hair.

"Do you think your aunt could have accidentally locked her in the closet?"

"No, no way," Zelda said. Her eyes went wide. "Aunt Bea would never ever treat Petunia like that, and she wasn't senile, if that's what you mean. Her mind was pretty sharp for her age."

Six

"Well, I doubt she locked herself in the closet," Ed said. Everyone stared at him, mouths agape. He went on hurriedly, "She looks like a smart cat, but I don't think she could have reached up and turned that little knob that locks the door."

"Well, she *was* in the closet, and it *was* locked," Zelda said. She glared at Ed.

"I do not doubt you, Ms. Terwilliger; I'm just stating a fact."

She made an 'hmph' sound, but her glare softened, just the tiniest bit. "It *sounded* like you doubted me," she said. "And, please, don't call me *Ms.* Terwilliger. I'm just Zelda. That's my stage name."

"Stage name?"

"Yeah, stage name. I'm the drummer for Tin Can Alley, a grunge band that plays clubs along the east coast."

"Tin Pan Alley?" Ed asked. "What's a grunge band?"

Zelda's glare turned into a kind of 'down-your-nose' look that is normally reserved for the really clueless. "Not Tin *Pan* Alley; Tin *Can* Alley. And, a grunge band is kind of a cross between heavy metal and punk, you know, like Nirvana."

Ed looked at her, his brown brow furrowed. The other three also looked confused. Zelda made a snorting sound.

"None of you have any idea what I'm talking about, do you?"

"Well," Ed said. "I know that nirvana is a Buddhist term that means freedom from suffering, or something like that."

She laughed. "I don't know anything about Buddhism, but Nirvana was a grunge band from the 90s, one of the most famous in fact. They brought grunge, which had been just scattered groups playing clubs in Seattle, Washington, into the mainstream. Anyway, I play the drums for Tin Can Alley. It doesn't like pay much, but it's better than the job I used to have. I was a mortuary cosmetologist. That's like, you know, the person who puts the makeup on stiffs after they get embalmed."

Ed held his hands up in surrender. "Okay, so you're a drummer in a band, and you no longer use your family name. I can work with that. If it's not music from the 60s and 70s I don't know much about it. What I'd like you to do, though, is to walk me through what happened Friday."

"The whole day?"

Ed sighed. He couldn't get over how difficult it seemed to be for some people to understand simple communication. She had to know he was concerned about what had happened to her aunt, so Zelda should have been able to intuit from that that he was mainly interested in the events at PVC after her arrival. Either she didn't understand that simple fact, or she was doing another thing people did that infuriated him—asking a question that she didn't really need the answer to. His curiosity, though, had invested him in the case, so he couldn't let his frustration show. He took a deep breath.

"No, just from the time you arrived here at PVC," he said, keeping his tone as pleasant as possible.

Zelda cocked her head to one side and narrowed her eyes while absently running her fingers through the hair on Petunia's stomach The cat, lolling on its back with its paws waving, glared at Ed as if upset that he was distracting Zelda from her main job, which was keeping it happy.

"Okay," Zelda finally said. "I got it. So, here's what happened. I was s'posed to come see Aunt Bea Thursday night, but, like, Tin Can Alley had a gig at Rockslide . . . that's this club up in Bowie . . . anyway, so like I called her and told her I couldn't make it, so she like told me to come for breakfast Friday."

Ed sat on the arm of the sofa near her.

"Did you visit your aunt often?"

"Uh, I dropped in on her like two or three times a month. I was by like last week, you know, but she wanted me to come back this week. Said she had something like real important to talk about."

"Oh, and what was that?"

"Aw, everything was important to Aunt Bea," she said. "I remember the time she like wanted to change Petunia's brand of cat food. She like called me to come over and discuss it."

Ed wanted to say 'pay attention, and answer my damn questions,' but instead he said, "Was it something trivial this time?"

"Nah, it was like pretty important, you know. She wanted to talk to me *and* Garfield about it."

"Who is Garfield?" Ed asked.

"Garfield's like my brother. He's five years older than me."

Too much information, Ed thought. "So, your aunt wanted to talk to the two of you?"

"Yeah, but not together. She wanted to talk to me first, and then to Garfield, which was kind of like strange I guess, but that was Aunt Bea, she liked to do things a certain way."

"Do you know if your brother visited her Thursday night?"

She shrugged. "I don't know. She said she wanted to talk to me first, but since I couldn't make it, she might've called him. You want I should like ask him?"

"No, I was just curious. Anyway, why don't you take me through what happened, step by step, and don't leave anything out." As soon as he said it, Ed regretted it.

"Well, I drove my bug; I got an old Volkswagen bug, it's mostly rust, but it used to be red; I drove it through the main gate. They made me wait while they checked to make sure I was on the authorized visitor list. Can you believe it? I mean, like, I come here to visit Aunt Bea . . . well, I used to visit her . . . a lot, so they oughta know me, right?"

Getting information from her was going to be like picking blackberries had been when he was a kid; you have to contend with a lot of weeds and thorns to get to the fruit. Losing patience with her wouldn't help, in all likelihood it would piss her off and cause her to clam up.

"Yeah, I know what you mean," he said. "But, they're just doing what they get paid to do. Say, Ernie, why don't you, Violet and Rose go out to the kitchen and start putting some food together while I talk to Zelda."

"Sure thing, amigo," Ernie said. "Come on ladies. Let's go rustle up some grub."

"Oh, Ernie," Rose said. "You have the quaintest way of putting things."

"Sounds like a hillbilly to me," Violet said.

Ernie smiled at the two women as he headed for the kitchen with them following.

"Violet, you shouldn't be so mean," Rose protested.

"That's okay, I know it's only 'cause she likes me."

Rose punched him playfully on the shoulder, while Violet snorted and pushed past them. Petunia, sensing that the three were going to some place interesting, flipped over and jumped off Zelda's lap and padded after them.

"Now, Zelda," Ed said. "You came through security and drove to your aunt's house. What happened after that?"

"Uh, I parked in the driveway like always, and then I like walked up and went in the front door. That's—"

"Didn't you ring the bell?" Ed interrupted her, causing her to frown.

` "No, I like used my key," she said with a trace of testiness. "Me and my brother both have keys. Sometimes when we visit, at least sometimes when I'd visit, she'd be sleeping, and she don't . . . didn't like for us to wake her up, so she gave us keys so we could just come in, you know, and wait until she woke up."

"Okay, I see. That makes sense. So, you let yourself in. What happened next?"

"At first I didn't see her. That's because she was lying on her side on the sofa. But, when I stepped inside the living room, I saw her lying there. I thought she was sleeping, you know. But, when I got closer I could tell she was . . . I mean, her lips were like sorta blue and her eyes were open. I saw enough corpses when I used to work in the funeral home to know a dead body when I see one." Tears welled up in her eyes and began making little trails down her cheeks.

Ed reached over and patted her hand.

"I'm sorry. I know this must be hard on you. If you want to stop, I'll understand."

"No, that's okay. I need to tell somebody, and Violet said you'd be the best person to tell. I mean, like something has to be done."

"Do you need help in making the final arrangements or anything?"

"It's not that. It's that Dr. Vickers sayin' that Aunt Bea died of a heart attack. I think he's fulla shit. My aunt was as healthy as a horse, and she didn't have any history of heart problems. I mean, sure, she was like old and all, and she was redoing her will, but she wasn't like sick or anything."

"Well," Ed said. "There's a simple enough way to confirm Dr. Vickers' diagnosis, but first, you say your aunt was doing a new will?"

"Yeah, that's why she wanted to talk to me and Garfield."

"What changes was she making?"

"I don't know. I guess that's what she like wanted to tell us. I guess we'll find out when the will's read, right?"

"I imagine so. Now, back to the cause of death," Ed said. "If you disagree with Dr. Vickers' diagnosis, you can always ask for someone to examine the body to establish a firm cause of death."

She put a hand over her mouth. "How do I do that?"

"Why . . . uh, I'm not really sure." Ed realized that he hadn't really thought it all the way out. "I'll look into that for you and let you know. My friend Ernie knows people who work in county government, maybe one of them can tell us how to do it."

"Thanks, that would help, I guess. When can he do it?"

"I'll ask him to do it first thing tomorrow," Ed said. "You need to let the mortuary know so the body can be moved to wherever such examinations are done."

"Yeah, I'll do that Monday," she said. "Violet and Rose said you were the only person here who could help me. It looks like they were right about that. Thanks, thanks a lot."

"I haven't done anything yet."

Seven

Ed found Zelda fascinating, in a somewhat bizarre and slightly irritating sort of way, but she seemed to be truthful. Over toasted tuna sandwiches and potato salad, washed down with lemonade made with freshly squeezed lemons, more details came out.

Of course, having to do that while eating, dealing with the efforts of Ernie, Violet, and Rose to be a part of the conversation, Petunia slinking between them from person to person begging for table scraps, and Zelda's inability to give a direct answer to a question, it was anything but easy.

"Zelda," Ed said. "When did you notice that Petunia was locked in the closet?"

Zelda lifted the top slice bread off her sandwich and rearranged the lettuce and tomato slices so that the lettuce was on top, and then replaced the bread, mashing it down a bit. "There was this cup of tea and a teapot about half full as well on the coffee table," she said. "I guess Aunt Bea must have been having a cup of tea before bed, although she wasn't dressed for bed—she wasn't in her nightgown and robe like she is when she's ready for bed, she was wearing her work-in-the-yard clothes." She took a nibble from her sandwich, chewing it twenty times before swallowing. "I checked her pulse, but she was like dead, you know. So I took the cup and teapot to the kitchen, emptied and washed them, and put them on the sink next to the tea cup that was sitting there. Uh, what was your question again?"

Ed sighed. "When did you notice the cat was locked in the closet?"

"Oh, yeah . . . that was right after I checked for a pulse. I mean, I like knew she was dead just from looking at her, but you should always check the pulse, you know. Anyway, I'd checked her pulse and then I heard this kinda scratching sound. It was coming from the closet near the front door, so I like opened the door and there was poor little Petunia. She looked so scared, and kinda hungry and thirsty."

"What did you do next?"

"Well, Petunia dashed out of that closet and ran straight for the litter box. Poor thing, she whizzed for the longest time. That's how I know she'd been in there a while. Then she went to her food and water dish in the kitchen, but they were empty. I guess Aunt Bea forgot to fill them the night before," she said. "I filled her water dish, and gave her some cat food from a bag in the pantry." Petunia was trying to climb her leg, mewing and reaching for the sandwich in Zelda's hand. She broke off a corner of her sandwich and handed it down. "There you go, Petunia. Who's a good girl?" Busy wolfing down the food, the cat ignored her. "Petunia's good like that, you know. She only goes in her litter box. I mean, she'd been in the closet a long time, but she didn't make a mess, did you Petunia baby? No you didn't, 'cause you're a good girl."

It was at this point that Ed realized that Zelda was a wealth of information, useful and some, not so useful. She absorbed and remembered everything that happened, but her mind didn't have the filters to help her decide what piece of the information she knew was an appropriate response to a question, therefore, she simply divulged everything. Since she disclosed information in a totally haphazard manner, the best way, he intuited, to get information from her was to seek it in the same manner—haphazardly.

"Was Petunia's water dish dry?" he asked.

"Yeah, it was like dry as a bone. I filled it at the sink to give her a drink. That's when I noticed the teacup sitting on the counter. Aunt Bea always kept her stuff put away unless she had guests."

"Do you think she had a guest?"

"Like she must have, you know," she said. "Or, maybe she was expecting someone. Maybe the cup was there for me, since she'd invited me over."

"Yeah, but you'd told her you weren't coming over."

"Hey, that's right. So, it wouldn't have been for me. Well, no, it could have been. She might have set it out knowing I'd be coming by in the morning."

"So, you think she got up and prepared a pot of tea that morning?"

"Uh, no, that can't be right. Aunt Bea liked her tea hot, I mean like smokin' hot, you know, and the tea in the pot on the coffee table was cold. And, she wouldn't have locked Petunia in the closet that long. Besides, when I checked for her pulse, her body had already stiffened. Like rigor mortis had set in and her arm was completely stiff. That takes at least eight hours, you know, so she'd been dead since midnight at least."

"How do you know this?"

"I told you, I was a mortuary cosmetologist before I became a drummer. When I studied it, they explained that kind of stuff. You have to know it if you're gonna apply makeup to the remains properly. Bodies get stiff after they die, but then rigor passes and they get limber again. If a body comes in, it helps to know when the person died, so you know when you'll be able to do cosmetics or dress them."

"What was in your aunt's will?"

"I don't know what was in her new will, but in the old one, Garfield and I, as her only family, split her estate equally."

"Do you and Garfield visit her together often?"

"Nah, we used to when we were kids, right after our folks died in a fire at our farm over near Bowie, but then Garfield opened his auto shop, and he's been like busy, you know."

"What kind of changes do you think your aunt was making to her will?"

"That's what she said she was gonna tell me when I came over," she said. "Only, when I showed up she was like dead, you know, so she never told me."

"Well, it's probably not all that important," Ed said. "People get to be a certain age, they sometimes do odd things."

"Not my Aunt Bea." Zelda's cheeks reddened. "She might have been old, but there was nothing wrong with her mind. And, and that Dr. Vincent—"

"Vickers," Ed prompted.

"Yeah, whatever. Anyway, he said she like died of a heart attack. I don't believe it. Is he even a real doctor? Aunt Bea's never been sick a day in her life. She couldn't have died of a heart attack."

Ed had no great faith in Vickers' ability as a doctor, but he had no reason to think that he'd make a mistake like that. He decided to let that remark slide.

And so, it went on like that for the hour it took them to finish the potato salad, another ten minutes while the five of them cleaned things up, and thirty minutes more outside on Ed's patio sipping lemonade from a second pitcher that Rose was kind enough to make. Ed wasn't at all sure he had enough information from among the tons of information that had spewed willy-nilly from Zelda in response to his equally willy-nilly questions, but he *was* sure that things were not as they seemed.

The thing that stood out was the cat in the closet. He wasn't a cat person, but Petunia was a well-behaved feline who seemed to get along with everyone and in his experience, cat people were not prone to abusing their pets. One had only to see how Violet, not the most easygoing person in the world, got along with the animal. That left the question, then, how did Petunia get locked in the closet? Who put her there? And, why? If only Petunia could talk, the story she might tell.

Eight

"So, we have ourselves a mystery, do we?" Ernie asked, staring at Ed over his coffee cup.

It was a slow Monday morning in the community center's dining room, and they'd had no trouble getting Ed's favorite table near the window, although, when the Ahearn brothers, who'd come in a few minutes behind them, had glared at them as they made their way to an empty table near the breakfast buffet line. The twin glares, though, were the only move made at them, for which Ed was grateful. He had too much on his mind to deal with petty nuisances like the Ahearns. They'd eaten a hearty breakfast, and then lingered over their second cups of coffee just to rub it in the Ahearn's faces.

Ed gazed down at his coffee, which had sat on the table untouched for several minutes.

"Maybe, but I'm not sure. Something doesn't smell right about the whole thing, frankly, but I can't quite put my finger on what it is."

"Well, she was an old lady. There's nothing odd about an old person croaking from a bum ticker. I mean, Zelda seems like a nice kid, a bit odd, but nice, and of course she'd be upset that her aunt died."

"True that, but there's the cat being locked in the closet. You have to admit that's a bit on the odd side."

Ernie took a drink of coffee, and then put his cup down, wrapping his hands around it.

"I guess so, but think about it Ed . . . Beatrice was old, she might have accidentally locked the cat in the closet."

"According to Zelda, the old lady had all her marbles. I can't imagine she'd be living here all alone if she was senile."

Ernie lifted his hands from the cup and rubbed them together.

"This just keeps getting better and better. So, that means someone else locked the cat up."

"I think that's what I just said," Ed said. "The question is, who?"

"I take it you and I are gonna find out, right?"

"Do you see anyone else here to do it?"

"So, what do we do first?" Ernie was smiling like a kid on Christmas morning.

"Well, Zelda said her aunt was healthy. I think we should ask Vickers if he's absolutely sure she died of a heart attack."

"I can go along with that. I never did trust that quack. We goin' to see him now?"

Ed looked around. The Ahearns sat hunched over their food, but their eyes were on Ed and Ernie.

"In a few minutes," Ed said. "I want to sit here and enjoy watching the Ahearn boys stew."

Ernie's loud laugh caused the Ahearns to scowl deeper and hunch lower over their food. Ed waited until it looked like Peter Ahearn would choke on his food. Slowly, he finished his coffee, stood, and took the empty cup to the shelf near the kitchen where stacks of dirty dishes, glasses, and cups waited for the kitchen staff to take them back for cleaning. They had to walk past the Ahearns' table going and coming. On the way back, Ed smiled down at them. They glowered back.

"Have a nice morning, boys," Ernie said.

What they murmured in return was unintelligible, but Ed guessed it would have been bleeped out if they'd said it on anything but cable TV.

They made their way to the reception hall and took the arched doorway on the left opposite the desk that led into the administrative wing and medical clinic.

For the convenience of PVC's elderly

residents, the clinic was at the front. The head nurse, Candice Drummond, had a tiny office at the head of the hallway, next to the examination room. Drummond, not one of Ed's favorite people since she'd endangered Violet's life when she'd been kidnapped, sat behind her desk, hunched over a brown folder. She looked up as Ed and Ernie passed, but when she saw who it was, looked quickly down at the papers on her desk, which made Ed smile. He supposed he'd have to go in one day and let her know that he was ready to forgive her for what she did, which, in retrospect was probably the proper thing to do, except she'd gotten the information from eavesdropping outside Vickers' office. Nah, he thought, let her squirm a few more weeks.

They passed two more doors, one of which Ed knew was the office Vickers used whenever he was in the clinic, and came to the entrance to the administrative wing.

The area should have been called the Roland Vickers Commemorative Wing, because it was less a center for the administration of Potomac Valley Community than a monument to the CEO's huge ego.

It was twice the size of the clinic, with two small offices flanking the entrance, one for PVC's accountant/bookkeeper and the other for the property manager who took care of day-to-day activities of the sprawling community. Beyond that was a large reception area with large aluminum containers of plants, and a few chairs grouped around low tables in what Vickers called 'intimate conversation areas' for the use of anyone visiting him. At the center of this, near the back, sat a metal and glass desk, behind which sat Lydia Myers, Vickers' personal assistant, a woman in her late twenties, who favored frilly, scooped neck blouses and skirts that ended well above mid-thigh. Her straw-colored hair draped down to her shoulders. She could have been considered beautiful, Ed thought as he and Ernie approached her desk, except for the fact that she was constantly chewing gum—with her mouth open—and studying her brightly colored fingernails with a vacant look in her sky blue eyes.

She stopped inspecting the glittery polish on her nails as they stopped in front of her desk.

"Yeah, how can I help you gentlemen?" Her tone didn't sound as if she really gave a fig what they wanted.

"We need to see Dr. Vickers," Ed said.

"Do you have an appointment?"

"No, we don't."

This was new. They had never needed an appointment to see Vickers before, but then, they'd never approached him in his CEO office before either.

"Sorry, if you don't have an appointment, you can't see Dr. Vickers. I can put you on his calendar, though, if you like."

The officious tone of her voice was off-putting enough, but the constant chewing between words set Ed's teeth on edge.

"When would the good doctor be available?" he asked.

She picked up a leatherette folder that lay on the desk at her elbow and opened it. After flicking idly through it for a few seconds, she snapped it shut and turned her sleepy gaze back to Ed.

"Would next Monday at 10:30 work for you?"

"Next Mon—, that's a week away!" He leaned forward, pressing his palms against the edge of her desk. "I can't believe he's that busy."

"Dr. Vickers *is* a very busy man." She didn't meet his eyes as she spoke.

No matter how provoked or angry he might become, Ed was not one to raise his voice. It might take on a sharp edge, but it was never raised much above a normal conversational level. Ernie, on the other hand, suffered under no such constraints. A barrel-chested man, when he stretched to his full height and puffed out his chest, he had the capacity to enormous volume. While he did not take full advantage of that volume when he leaned forward and glared down at Lydia Myers, who shrank back from his imposing physical presence, and positively shivered when his voice boomed out, "You mean he's too busy to give a few minutes to this community's most important resident! Why that's the most outrageous thing I've ever heard."

The young women's already sun-deprived face paled to an even sicklier shade of white and she shrank further back against her chair which was not pinned against the wall behind her desk. She looked like she was about to cry.

"I only need a few minutes of his time," Ed said, holding a hand up to restrain Ernie from a further outburst. "It's a matter of life or death."

The door to the right opened and Vickers stood in the doorway, framed by the light from his office.

"Really, Edward," he said. "And, just whose life or death would you be referring to?"

Unfazed, Ed took in the man's cold expression. "Could we talk privately in your office? It'll only take a few minutes," Ed said.

"You wouldn't want word to get around that you don't have a few minutes for residents, would you?" Ernie added.

Vickers blinked. He tugged at his left ear lobe.

"Why, I always have time for our valued residents," he said. He stepped aside and waved his right hand in a sweeping gesture. "Come in, please. Ms. Myers, hold all calls except for legitimate emergencies."

Looking confused, Myers nodded.

Once the door was closed, Vickers' aloof expression returned. He strode behind his desk and sat, waving idly at the two chairs placed in front of the desk, the straight back, uncomfortable kind of chair that one would expect to find in a vice principal's office at a particularly unruly high school.

Vickers steepled his hands and rested his chin on the tips of his fingers, looking at Ed and Ernie exactly the way Ed remembered the vice principal at his high school looking at him the time during his sophomore year he and a bunch of his buddies had cut class to go see a stock car race at the track on the outskirts of town. Back then, he'd been scared that his parents would be told and he'd end up being grounded until he graduated. Vickers, though, wasn't a vice principal, and there was no one around to ground him, even if he had done something wrong, which he hadn't.

"We need just a moment of your time, Dr. Vickers," he said. "It's very important."

"Yes, I believe you said it was a matter of life or death?"

Ed smiled and looked down at his hands, held clasped together in his lap. Realizing that he'd unconsciously adopted the posture of a student caught in the wrong he unclasped his hands and looked across the desk at Vickers.

"Well, it's more a matter of death than

life," he said. "Did Beatrice Terwilliger really die of a heart attack?"

Vickers' brows arched upwards and he lifted his chin off his fingertips.

"That is not a matter that I can discuss with anyone but a member of Ms. Terwilliger's family."

"Come on, doc," Ernie said before Ed could react. "We're all just one big family here, and it's not like you'd be violating a patient's confidence or anything, seeing as how she's already dead."

"It doesn't matter," Vickers said. "I don't feel comfortable discussing even a deceased patient with people who have no relationship."

What Ed knew about the ethics of the medical profession could be crammed into his eye without causing irritation, but he sensed that Vickers was just being bureaucratic. In that regard he was a lot like some of the bureaucrats Ed had dealt with during his years working at the Pentagon; always using 'need to know' as an excuse to withhold information, even when it wasn't classified.

"Dr. Vickers, you know as well as I do that the rumor mill around this place operates overtime. People will be talking about this situation, and all kinds of theories will be floating around. If you could just confirm that it was a heart attack, Ernie and I can help to forestall a lot of unnecessary gossip,"

Ed said. This was a ploy he'd used on more than one occasion. Making it seem that he was on the bureaucrat's side, and would be helpful, appealed to the basic selfish nature of people.

The way Vickers' eyes narrowed for a microsecond told him that the man was thinking the same thing.

"I suppose you have a point," Vickers said. "It is unfortunate that the residents here seem to have so little to occupy their time. Very well, but you're to repeat this only if the subject comes up. Beatrice Terwilliger did indeed expire due to a coronary event . . . heart attack."

"Are you sure?"

Now, Vickers' eyes narrowed for longer than a microsecond, and his lips turned down. "Are you questioning my medical diagnosis, Ed? I've been a doctor for over twenty-five years, and I recognize the symptoms of a heart attack when I see them. Beatrice Terwilliger was an elderly woman, and slightly overweight. She was a prime candidate for a heart attack or a stroke."

"Not questioning your expertise," Ed said. "I was just wondering if there was something else that could have killed her that would look like a heart attack."

Vickers smiled. "Ah, the amateur detective is at it again, eh? Sure, there are some toxins that can mimic heart attacks, but there were no signs of trauma to her body, and she was alone in her residence except for her cat. From the state of rigor, she'd been dead for some time before her niece found her. She was probably having tea when her heart gave out. I can assure you she died peacefully of a heart attack. Now, if there's nothing else you need, I *am* quite busy this morning."

Ed looked at the man's desk. Except for his blotter and a gold Parker pen set, it was bare. His inbox and outbox were both empty, and the area outside his office was vacant except for Lydia Myers who'd looked anything but busy. He knew they were being given the bums' rush, but he could think of nothing else to ask. He had, though, to at least get in a parting shot.

"Sure, Dr. Vickers," he said. "Thanks for your time. By the way, you really ought to tell your secretary to be a little nicer to residents who want to see you. She tried to put us off by setting an appointment for a week from now. Some of the folks here might be a bit miffed at such treatment."

"Yes, Lydia . . . Ms. Myers means well. She's only been working for me for a couple of months now, and she's still getting to know the place. I will, of course, talk to her about her people skills."

He stood as he spoke, sending a clear signal that the meeting was over. Ed was pretty certain that he wouldn't say anything to Myers. But, he had someone else he wanted to talk to anyway, so he nodded at

Ernie, and without offering to shake hands, the two of them rose and left the office.

Lydia Myers was still chewing her gum and studying her fingernails as they walked past her desk. She didn't even bother to look up at them as they passed.

Nine

They walked in silence back to Ed's house, neither speaking until they were standing in Ed's kitchen. Ernie leaned on the counter as Ed prepared a pot of coffee.

"So, amigo," Ernie said. "What do we do now?"

Ed stopped what he was doing and turned to face his friend.

"Tell me, Ernie, do you trust Zelda? Do you think she was telling us the truth when she said her aunt was healthy and unlikely to have had heart problems?"

"Yeah," Ernie said after a screwing up his face in concentration for a couple of seconds. "She's a little strange, but she didn't strike me as anything else but truthful."

"If Bea Terwilliger didn't die from a heart attack, something else killed her. What we have to do is found out what, and who did it."

"Huh?"

"Look, I didn't know the woman, but she doesn't strike me as someone who would kill herself. Hell, if she was healthy, what would have been the reason?"

"You're sayin' you think someone killed her?"

"Right now, I'm just saying 'what if.' Until we know how she really died, there's nothing we can say."

"How we gonna find that out?"

"I thought I'd give a call to someone who just might be able to help us do that."

Ernie looked confused, and then his mouth dropped open. "You don't mean you're gonna call—"

"That's right, old friend," Ed said. "If anyone can tell us how to do it, Detective Carl Janzen can."

Ernie shook his head. "I know he was friendly enough with us the last time we crossed paths, but I still don't think he likes it when we stick our noses into police business."

That was true. Although Ed's last encounter with the Montgomery County cop had been cordial enough, there had also been a bit of an edge to Janzen's voice when he warned Ed and Ernie to 'stay out of trouble.' How much of that warning had been because of friendship and how much from a normal police aversion to civilians interfering with police investigations, Ed didn't know. What he did know, though, was that he needed some expert advice on how to proceed in the present case, and Janzen was the only 'expert' he knew. He hoped that the man would understand. After all, this wasn't a police case—yet. There were no signs of foul play, just Zelda's belief that her aunt hadn't died of a heart attack. She could be wrong about that, and maybe Janzen could tell Ed how he could go about convincing her.

With Ernie looking on skeptically, he flipped open his last-generation cell phone and dialed the number Janzen had given him the first time they met. It was to the precinct in which Janzen worked, and a youthful sounding female voice answered on the third ring.

"Montgomery County Police Department, Investigative Section," the voice said. "How may I direct your call?"

"May I speak to Detective Carl Janzen?" Ed asked.

The voice then put Ed through a series of questions; name, purpose of call, is this an emergency, to which he answered, Ed Lazenby, a request for assistance, and no it wasn't an emergency.

"Is there anyone else who can help you?"

"No, I don't think so," Ed replied. "I know Detective Janzen, and would feel more comfortable talking to him. If he's busy, I can give you my number. Could you ask him to call me as soon as he's free?" He tried not to let his impatience sound in his voice.

After a few seconds of silence, the cheery voice came back on the line. "Please hold, I'll transfer you to Detective Janzen's number."

Ed heard a beeping sound, and then elevator music filled his ear. Thankfully, a few seconds later, Janzen's booming voice echoed in his ear.

"Janzen here," he said. "Ed Lazenby? You're not in some kind of trouble are you?"

Ed chuckled. "No, I'm not into or up to any trouble, Carl," he said. "But, I have a friend who has a problem . . . well, more like a question, and it's kind of technical. I was hoping you could help me answer it for her."

Ed heard Janzen's throaty chuckle. "Her, huh? Sounds like you have a nice kind of problem. New girlfriend has an ex she's worried about?"

"It's not like that, really. This person's young enough to be my granddaughter. You know me, though; when someone has a problem I like to help them if I can."

"Okay, if you say so, what's her . . . question?"

Ed then explained the situation, starting with learning of Beatrice Terwilliger's death and his conversation with Zelda, leaving out the part about the cat in the closet.

"Sounds like a pretty cut and dried case to me," Janzen said when he'd finished. "It's not unusual for old people to die from heart attacks. I think that you of all people would understand that, given the age range of your neighbors. Anyway, if a doctor was present at the death and certified the cause, it's not a police matter, so I don't know how I can help you."

"What if a family member disagrees with the doctor's diagnosis?"

"Well, a cause of death's not exactly a diagnosis, but if the family thinks it was different than what the doctor determined, they can always ask that an autopsy be conducted. It'd take time, but they could call the county medical examiner and ask for one."

"I knew you'd be able to help. Thanks, Carl."

"Don't mention it, Ed." Janzen chuckled again. "Now go put that help to good use . . . but, please, try and stay out of trouble."

"You know I will."

"Yeah, right. I seem to remember you saying that a time or two in the past, and we both know how that worked out, don't we?"

Charles Ray

Ten

"What'd he say, what'd he say? Come on, tell me what he told you," Ernie said, sounding like a child trying to talk his father into buying him that new American Flyer bike in the toy department, the one that costs a lot more than dad's prepared to pay.

Ed held his hands up in a traffic cop's 'stop' gesture. "He told me that Zelda should request the county to do an autopsy."

Ernie's face drooped in a dejected expression.

"That's it? Surely there's something else . . . something a little more interesting we can do."

"Nope, that's it. Now, if you'll be quiet a minute, I need to call Zelda and give her the news."

Ernie sat back on the sofa with his arms folded across his chest and a schoolboy pout on his face. Ed flipped open his phone and keyed in the number Zelda had given him.

"Hello," her voice said after two rings.

"Zelda, this is Ed Lazenby. I just talked to a friend of mine who is with the police, and he said you can request an autopsy to definitely determine the cause of your aunt's death."

"Uh . . . how do I do that?"

"He said you have to call the county medical examiner," Ed said.

"Who do I ask for? What do I say to them?"

The whine in her voice grated on Ed, but he held his irritation in check. "I suppose you talk to whoever answers the phone, or ask them," he said slowly. "And, you ask them for the forms to request an autopsy be performed on your recently deceased aunt."

"Uh, I don't know," she said. "I'm not good talking to people on the phone, especially government types." She paused as if waiting for Ed to volunteer to do it for her. After ten seconds of silence, her whining voice came back on. "I guess I could ask Garfield to do it. He's taking care of everything else."

"Who is Garfield?" Ed asked.

"You remember, I told you before. He's my brother. He's three years older than me. He's been taking care of the arrangements for Aunt Bea. He even did little jobs for her whenever I was touring with the band, not often, just when she needed something that couldn't wait until I got back. He didn't like going to her place, said it smelled too much like old people. Considering that he works in a stinky garage, that's like rich, don't you think?"

A glimmer of a thought winked into existence in the rearmost recess of Ed's mind. But, thanks to Zelda's rambling, it disappeared before he could quite get hold of it, but he did grab onto the idea that he should have a talk with Zelda's brother—just to satisfy his curiosity.

"I'd like to speak with him," he said. "Where can I reach him?"

"Probably at his garage." She gave him an address on Georgia Avenue, not far from where it intersected with Norbeck Road. "Could you ask him to call about the autopsy when you talk to him?"

Ed took in a deep breath. If this Garfield was as averse to doing anything as his sister, it should be an interesting meeting. Ed's way of handling clingy, dependent people, though, was simple—he refused to facilitate their lack of grit. "No, I think that's something that should come from you. Imagine how you'd feel if a total stranger came up to you and suggested you get an autopsy on your aunt. How would you feel?"

"I'd probably ask them how to do it."

"Well, in this case, I'm suggesting very strongly that *you* call your brother right away and tell him to request that autopsy."

Before she could protest, Ed broke the

connection.

"I could tell from you end of the conversation that Zelda's a piece of work," Ernie said. "So, what do we do now?"

"We're going to a garage."

Eleven

Over Ernie's protests, they took Ed's Toyota 4-Runner for the drive to the address Zelda had given him. Ernie argued that a pickup was *the* vehicle to take to a garage in that it would impress the motor heads who hung out in such places, but Ed countered with the argument that they wanted to appear harmless which would be more likely to make Garfield Terwilliger to talk to them, and a pickup was too aggressive. He finally said that he was the one who knew the address to which they were driving, and he'd rather just drive straight there instead of having to ride shotgun and give directions. Ernie huffed and puffed, and pouted a bit, but Ed stuck to his guns until his friend relented.

Westbound traffic on Norbeck Road was light when they left PVC around mid-afternoon, but they still had to wait several minutes for a break in the eastbound flow of people leaving work early and heading for their homes in northeastern Montgomery County and southwestern Howard County. As they sat there, Ed pondered complaining about it to Violet, which would be sure to get her started on another of her campaigns to 'improve' life in PVC, this time, arguing for a traffic light at their main entrance. It was a campaign that he was pretty sure stood a snowball's chances of transiting hell without losing weight, but it might be entertaining to see Violet forcing local officials to jump through hoops trying find a politically correct way to turn her down.

When Ed was finally able to make the left turn, he signaled and began easing to the right, just narrowly missing getting clipped by a little old lady in a Prius who'd tried to slip around him without signaling her intention to change lanes. As she zipped past him, stabbing at her horn, she glared at him, mouthing words he couldn't make out because her window was closed as was his, but he was pretty sure he was being told to do something to himself that was physically impossible. Her shrugged and smiled at her, but she was going too fast to react. After she was half a car length ahead, he moved over to the far right.

"See, if we'd been driving my pickup, that old biddy would never have pulled a stunt like that," Ernie said.

"You have got to be kidding." Ed made a snorting noise. "You know damn good and well she would have done the same thing. The difference is, in your pickup, we might not have been able to maneuver quickly enough to keep from hitting her."

Ernie shrugged and hunched down with his forehead against the window. Ed made a growling sound. He wondered why he ever engaged his friend in the 'pickup versus any other kind of car' debates, because Ernie was convinced that the only vehicle for a real man to drive was a pickup, preferably a double-cab truck with racing tires and roll bars. It came, he always told Ed, from having driving the puny little mail van for so many years. With its right-hand side drive, and flimsy appearance, it was intimidated by everything with four wheels, and quite a few of the larger Harley-Davison two-wheelers. Now, in his retirement, Ernie was determined never again to be beaten on the road.

Fortunately, they made the rest of the journey to Georgia Avenue without incident. They got the green light at the intersection and Ed made the right turn onto the busy thoroughfare. He began scanning to his right for Zelda's brother Garfield's garage.

He almost missed it.

The faded sign, a large stained piece of white metal almost covered by weeds, said *'Garfield's Garage – You wreck 'em, we fix 'em'* in black ink on a chipped white and rust metal rectangle—more rust than white. The weeds crawled halfway up the rusty chain link fence that enclosed a graveled rectangle in the middle of which sat a rusty corrugated metal building that was more red from rust than its original silver color. The metal gate hung half off its hinges and sagged in the middle. Half of the front of the building was taken up by a huge metal rollup door that was in the up position. 'Garfield's Garage' was painted in faded blue script above the door. The area around the front and sides of the building was littered with cars in various phases of disassembly, from only tires missing to almost everything stripped, leaving skeletons sitting on concrete blocks like some gaunt monsters crouching awaiting their prey, or perhaps more appropriately, prey after all the good parts have been eaten by some voracious hunter.

Ed parked his 4-Runner in the most open space he could find, which was, unfortunately, a good fifty yards from the gaping entrance to the building, which meant that he and Ernie had to thread their way past scattered auto parts and rusted out hulks of cars that had long been stripped of everything useful. He was careful not to touch anything, thinking that all he needed was to get cut by some jagged piece of metal and get tetanus from whatever the gray-green gunk was that coated much of the exposed metal.

"The motto of this place oughta be, 'you wreck 'em, and we finish 'em off.' You ever see so many stripped down hulks in your life?" Ernie said.

"Yeah, in a junkyard," Ed responded.

By the time they'd walked up the concrete ramp to the concrete pad surrounding the building, Ed was regretting having parked so far away. Despite the gravel covering the lot, they'd kicked up dust as they walked, and his shoes and trouser legs were coated with a light brown dust that he knew would be hard to get out.

A gray van covered with rust spots, and with 'Garfield's Garage' and a 240 area code phone number painted in black on the side, was parked to the right of the door. Not exactly a good advertisement for his services, Ed thought.

"What do you call this?" Ernie asked innocently.

Ed looked around and shrugged. There was no answer to that. The place did, in fact, look like a junkyard rather than a repair facility.

They walked through the doorway. Inside, the cavernous space was lined with six repair pits and hoists, with large wheeled diagnostic machines beside them. An assortment of tools hung on pegs on the right wall. The smell of gasoline, grease and oil hung heavily in the still air. Large circular light fixtures hung suspended from the roof girders over each pit, along with the light coming through the open door, providing the only illumination. Three of the repair hoists had cars on them, late model cars with doors and other parts removed, but otherwise looking to be in good condition.

A small office, little more than a ten by ten box about eight feet high with a door on one side and a window on the other, was stuck in the left rear corner of the building. Black electric wired ran down the building wall and into the top of the office.

The place was quiet, only the sound of their footsteps on the concrete floor as they approached the office. As they came closer, they could see movement through the window, but the accumulation of grease and dirt made it impossible to see more than a shadow.

Ed walked up and rapped on the flimsy wooden door.

After a few seconds, there was a squeaking sound from inside the office, then footsteps on the wooden floor, and the door swung inward.

The man who stood in the door was about five-six, and probably weighed one-sixty. He wore a pair of gray coveralls and steel-toed work boots. Even without the name 'Garfield' embroidered in red ink over his left breast, Ed could see the resemblance to Zelda, but his features were much sharper, with an unfriendly stare in his eyes.

"Yeah, what can I do for you?" he asked. His tone was as unwelcoming as the look in his eyes. "If you need repairs, I can't help you. I'm booked pretty solid right now, but I can recommend a garage over in Rockville on Viers Mill Road."

Ed looked around at the quiet space, with cars sitting on racks not being worked on, and with no one else in the place. Unless he was a one-man operation, or he gave exceptionally long lunch hours, he certainly didn't look all that busy.

"I'm not here for repairs," Ed said. "You're Garfield Terwilliger, I take it?"

"Yeah, who wants to know?"

"My name's Ed Lazenby and this is my friend, Ernesto Cardoza. We were neighbors of our aunt Beatrice Terwilliger at Potomac Valley Community."

"Well, if my aunt owed you money or anything, you'll have to submit the bill to the lawyer and wait until the will's probated."

"I'm not here about money, young man," Ed said. While Zelda had trouble coming to the point, her brother seemed to fix on a nonexistent point and glom right onto it. "We spoke with your sister, Zelda, and she was a bit worried that maybe the doctor made a mistake when he said your aunt died of a heart attack."

Terwilliger's eyes narrowed. "Zelda's a bit flaky. Aunt Bea was an old lady, and old people die from heart trouble all the time. If the doctor said it was a heart attack, that's what it was. What's it got to do with you two comin' here?"

The man's truculent attitude was beginning to irritate Ed. "We were just wondering if you have any reason to think your aunt might *not* have had a heart attack?"

"How the fuck should I know," he said. "If the doctor said it was a heart attack, that's good enough for me. Why the hell are you two sticking your noses in this anyway?" As he spoke, flecks of spittle flew from his mouth causing Ed to step backwards to keep from being sprayed.

Ed looked at the young man, taking in his harsh voice and the glare on his face. A certain amount of anger he could understand and accept, after all, he'd just lost his aunt. But, he was only willing to go so far—or to allow Garfield to go so far. He took a deep breath before speaking.

"We spoke with your sister," he said. "She had some concerns about the doctor's diagnosis, and asked if we'd look into it. Did your aunt have any health issues that you're aware of?"

Terwilliger's frown deepened. His eyes darted from side to side, not quite looking *at* either of them, but at spots to their sides.

"What're you, some kind of private detective?" His expression said he found that hard to believe.

"No," Ed said. "I'm just a concerned friend. Your sister asked for help, and that's what we're trying to do."

"So, you're not a PI, a lawyer or a cop, right?"

"That is correct."

"Then, get the fuck out of here and leave me alone. And, keep your fuckin' noses out of my family's business." He stepped back and slammed the door.

Ernie looked at Ed with a puzzled frown on his face.

"Now," Ed said. "That was interesting, interesting indeed."

Charles Ray

Twelve

It was late when Ed and Ernie got back to PVC, so they went straight to the community center for supper. Violet and Rose were already there, occupying their favorite window-side table and smiling innocently at the Ahearns, who were again forced to take a table near the entrance to the kitchen and, from the looks on their faces, unhappy about it as usual.

"Looks like you two are beginning to enjoy twitting the Ahearn boys a bit too much," Ed said as he and Ernie joined them. "But, I do thank you for saving our table."

"It's got nothing to do with saving you a table," Violet said. "It's that those two irritate me with their insufferable attitudes, so it pleases me to piss them off."

Rose blushed. "I don't normally go along with Violet antagonizing people, but they *are* quite arrogant in their behavior, and so nosey."

"Nosey, nosey in what way?" Ed asked.

"Why, haven't you noticed? They're always prowling around, peeking into people's backyards and such. It's really a nuisance. I think once they even came up and peeked into our living room window."

"Well, Peeping Patrick and Peeping Peter," Ernie said. "Say, Ed, maybe we should start a neighborhood watch and see if we can catch them in the act."

"Oh, they're nuisances, but they can't be all that bad. Come on, let's go get our food."

"No, Rose is right," Violet said as they stood. "They are always prowling around the neighborhood. In fact, I saw them near Bea's house the morning they found her dead."

"Really?" Ed said. He stopped and turned to face her. "You don't think they might have sneaked into her house and killed her, do you?" He turned his head and winked at Ernie.

Violet made a snorting sound and curled her lips down. Violet put her hand over her mouth to stifle a giggle. "You mock all you want, Ed Lazenby," Violet said. "I'm not saying they'd kill anybody, but I think Rose is right. I think they're a couple of peeping Toms."

"Well, in that case, you'd better remember to keep your curtains closed." Ed chuckled, turned and resumed his journey toward the buffet display.

"Violet's a pain in the ass," Ernie said. "But, neither she nor Rose is given to exaggeration. If they say the Ahearn boys been peeping, I'm inclined to agree with 'em. Maybe we ought to have a little chat with them."

"Just what I was thinking," Ed said quietly.

The Ahearns switched from glaring at Violet and Rose to watching Ed and Ernie warily as they slowly crossed the room, angling more at their table than the buffet line, with their glares changing to looks of apprehension.

Four feet from the table, Ed stopped so suddenly, Ernie bumped into him.

"Oops, sorry," Ernie said. "Give me a heads up next time you decide to put on the brakes."

Ed ignored him, his intention focused on Patrick and Peter Ahearn.

"Evening fellows," he said. "How are you this fine evening?"

The Ahearns exchanged puzzled looks. "We're doing fine," they finally both muttered almost under their breath.

"We hear you two've been wandering around the community," Ernie said. "Visiting people's backyards and maybe peeking into their bedroom windows?"

Their brows arched up and their eyes went wide. They looked at each other and then back at Ernie and Ed.

"Ridiculous," Peter Ahearn said.

"We're not voyeurs," Patrick added.

They both looked over at Violet and Rose.

"Who told you such a scandalous thing?" Peter asked.

Ed stepped forward and lowered his voice.

"It doesn't matter," he said. "Just don't let us catch you prowling around anyone else's house, got it?"

"B-but, we're amateur lepidopterists," Peter said.

"Lepidwhatsiwists?" Ernie asked.

"It means they study butterflies and moths," Ed said.

Peter nodded vigorously. "That's right, and this community is right on the migration routes of the monarch butterfly and the gypsy moth. They're just beginning to move now, and we *have* to catalog their numbers."

Ernie slapped his head to his brow. "You mean you two been sneakin' 'round people's backyards counting bugs?"

Patrick made a 'hmph' sound and tilted his head back, regarding Ernie down his prominent nose. "They're not bugs, you cretin," he said. "They are members of the insect order Lepidoptera, the second largest in the insect class. The monarch is currently under threat from use of insecticides, so it's important to keep track of the numbers. As for the gypsy moth, we just find it an interesting specimen."

"What's a cretin?" Ernie asked.

Ed punched his shoulder and pushed him gently toward the buffet line. "Don't worry about it," he said. "Let's get our food." He looked back at the Ahearns. "Okay, sorry if we wrongly accused you, boys."

Ernie was still mumbling and crinkling his brow as they put plates on plastic trays and began filling them from the food on display. "I think he insulted me, Ed," he said. "I should go back and smack him up side his head."

"If you did that, my friend, you'd only prove him right. Be the bigger man and ignore it."

Ernie was only slightly mollified, but he turned his attention to the food, and began piling his plate high with fried chicken, mashed potatoes, baby carrots and corn muffins. Ed copied him, only taking a slightly smaller amount. After ordering glasses of iced tea from the skinny, hairnet-wearing woman at the beverage counter, they returned to join Violet and Rose.

"Well, was I right?" Violet asked. "Have they been prowling around people's yards?"

"You were," Ed replied, but for the wrong reason. They're bug watchers, cataloging butterflies and moths, not peeking into your bedroom."

"That may be so." She sniffed. "But, they still give me the creeps."

"Did you talk to Zelda today?" Rose asked.

"Yeah, and I talked to Detective Janzen, too. He suggested she ask the county to do an autopsy to check Dr. Vickers' finding, so I passed that along to her."

Rose toyed with the string beans on her plate, stacking them, knocking them over, and restacking them. "That should allay her concerns, I hope."

"Me too," Ed said. He scrunched his eyes and wrinkled his brow.

"You look concerned." Rose had noted his expression.

"Ernie and I visited her older brother at his garage today. I don't know what it is exactly, but something about him bothers me."

"You mean other than the fact that he's an impolite little turd," Ernie said around a mouthful of food.

Ed nodded. "Yes, other than that."

Thirteen

After supper, Ed and Ernie offered to walk the Wertheim sisters to their house. Half a block from their destination, Rose's phone rang. She took it from her purse and answered.

"Rose Wertheim," she said. She listened for a while, a puzzled look on her face, and then said, "Yes, dear, of course . . . first thing in the morning . . . I'm sure that would be fine . . . we'll see you then." She thumbed off the phone and put it back in her purse.

"Well, aren't you going to share it with us?" Violet asked.

"Oh, yes . . . that was Zelda. She sounded quite upset. Said she needed to talk to us right away, but she's in Baltimore tonight playing at some club . . . she'll come in the morning for breakfast." She looked at Ed. "Could you and Ernie come to our house for

113

breakfast? She specifically said that she'd like to talk to you too, Ed."

"Of course, Rose. What did she say the problem was?"

"She didn't say, but she sounded quite upset."

They'd continued to walk as Rose talked on the phone, and had arrived in front of the house.

"Well then, I guess we'll see you ladies in the morning," Ed said. "Come on, Ernie, how about a nightcap before we turn in."

"I won't say no to that. Night, Rose, night, Violet," Ernie said.

The little nightcap turned into half a bottle of vodka, and Ed woke up at 6:00 the next morning with a pounding in his head that would have rivaled an artillery barrage. So much for vodka being the one drink that didn't cause hangovers, he thought as he pressed the heels of his hands to his pounding temples. After a few seconds the pounding eased, and he made his way to the bathroom, where he splashed his face with cold water. After a lukewarm shower he felt almost human again, and was at least steady enough to pull on a pair of jeans and a polo shirt, but he didn't feel up to lacing shoes, so he slipped his bare feet into a pair of sandals, and left the house.

Ernie, looking as bad as Ed felt, was just walking up the sidewalk. "You look like death warmed over," Ernie said.

"Not so loud, please," Ed said, holding his hands up, palms out. "I hope Violet has a pot of coffee ready."

"I'd say let's walk fast, but the sound of our footsteps would split my head."

It took them twice as long as usual to cover the distance from Ed's house to the Wertheim sisters' house. When he rang the doorbell, the echoing of the chimes, even from inside the house, ratcheted his headache up again. Next to him, Ernie winced at the sound as well.

Rose, with a beaming smile on her face, opened the door.

"Hi, guys," she said. "Come on in." She frowned as they limped past her. "Violet has a pot of coffee already made, and you two look like you need it."

"Is Zelda here yet?" Ed asked.

"No, she called a few minutes ago and said she was on her way."

"Well, in that case, I'll have a cup of Violet's coffee."

"Me too," Ernie said.

They followed her into the kitchen where Violet was stirring pancake batter and frying a skillet of bacon at the same time. On the counter near the sink, the large coffee maker was filled with coffee so dark it looked black instead of brown. Rose took two large ceramic cups from the cabinet and filled them with coffee, and handed them to the two men.

Then she poured coffee for herself into a smaller cup. Ernie grabbed the little white bowl of sugar from the center of the table and dumped the white granules into his cup without even measuring.

Ed and Ernie blew on the steaming liquid until they felt it was cool enough not to scald their mouths, and then began gulping it down, stopping only when the cups were half empty. Rose shook a finger at them, sloshing a bit of coffee as she did so.

"Honestly, I do not understand why you men drink the way you do," she said. "If something made me feel that way the next morning, I'd stay away from it."

Ed wanted to argue with her, but the dull pounding in his head—at least it wasn't so loud anymore—and the raspy feel of steel wool in his mouth made her words sound sensible. Besides, he thought, he didn't do it that often.

"I hope Zelda gets here soon," was all he could say. "I need something solid in my stomach to make the hangover go away."

As soon as the words were out of his mouth, the front doorbell rang. Rose put her cup on the kitchen table and scurried to the living room. She returned a few seconds later with Zelda in tow. The hang dog look on Zelda's face led Ed to conclude that the young woman had, like him and Ed, ended the night by searching for the bottom of a bottle of spirits.

"Good morning, Zelda," he said.

"Don't talk to me until I've had a cup of coffee," she muttered as she tottered toward the counter and grabbed the coffee pot. "Rose, where do you keep the cups?"

Rose rushed to her side and took a large white mug from the counter, and handed it to her. Zelda filled the mug, blew quickly on it and then put it to her lips. She tilted her head back and began chugging the coffee down with loud slurping noises that caused Rose to cringe. Ed looked on with a sympathetic expression. He'd been there before after a long evening of drinking with Ernie—hell, he was just coming back from there—so he knew how she felt. The way she looked made his hangover seem trivial.

When Zelda finished the coffee she lowered the cup and wiped her lips with the back of her hand. She then poured another cup and, cradling it against her breasts, she turned and leaned back against the counter.

"Good morning, everyone," she said, smiling wanly.

Violet mumbled something incoherent, Rose beamed, and Ernie nodded, leaving Ed to pick up the conversational slack.

"Good morning, Zelda," he said. "I take it you had a rough night."

"You could say that. We had a great gig up north, so we decided to like celebrate. I lost track of the bottles, but we didn't get back here until five this morning."

"My goodness, you must be tired, dear," Rose said. "Maybe you should rest."

Zelda put the mug on the counter and knuckled her eyes, yawning. "Oh, I'm okay now. That first cup of coffee gets my heart started. Man, did we really put one on last night . . . or this morning. We started drinking Wild Turkey, but by the time we stopped this morning, I was too drunk to read the label."

"Oh, dear," Rose said.

Ed didn't want Zelda to go off on another of her verbal side trips, so he stepped up close to her, close enough to detect the odor of sour liquor in her body sweat and on her breath.

"Do you feel up to talking about your aunt?" he asked.

"Sure. That's why I called and like asked to come over, you know. I talked to Aunt Bea's lawyer yesterday . . . well, I guess he's sort of my lawyer now, me being one of the inheritors of Aunt Bea's estate and all . . . and he told me about Aunt Bea's new will . . . which is missing, and he's not sure she signed it, so everything's kinda like a mess, you know."

Ed took a deep breath. Keeping her on track was going to be a challenge, and the dull pounding in his skull wasn't helping.

"So, what was in this new will?"

"Mr. Montrose . . . that's Aunt Bea's lawyer . . . wouldn't tell me. He said, until the will can be found he'd rather keep it confidential."

"Don't you have a clue?"

"Like if I had a clue, would I be asking him? No, I don't have a clue." She picked her mug up jerkily, and took a long swallow.

"Okay, so what's in the original will then?"

"Oh, that's easy; like I told you before, me and Garfield like split Aunt Bea's estate evenly."

Finally, Ed thought, she's focusing on the subject at hand and not rambling. "And, just what is that estate worth?"

"Gee, I'm not sure," Zelda said, tapping the end of her nose. "With her jewelry and junk, the bank accounts . . . oh, and the stock certificates, I think it's about five million."

"Dollars?" Ernie said, gulping.

"No, Pesos," Zelda said. "Of course dollars. What else would it be?"

"That's a lot of money. What do you plan to do with your share?"

She cocked her head to one side and tapped her nose again. "I hadn't really thought about it, you know. I guess maybe I'll like buy a new car, or fix my place up."

"What about your brother?" Ed asked. "What do you think he might do with his share?"

Her eyes narrowed, and her lips flickered in a quick frown before going back to her normal bored look. She breathed in and out slowly. Ed could tell she was mulling over an answer to his question, which surprised him, as until now she'd just blurted answers out without much thinking behind them. Finally, her gaze softened. Her face took on a sad, resigned look.

"If I know Garfield," she said. "Most of it'll go up his nose." At Ed's surprised look, she laughed. "I know what you're thinking, the odd looking one should be the one doing drugs, and Mr. Clean, owner of his own business should walk the straight and narrow, but that's not the way it rolls in this family. I probably drink a bit too much, but I've never used drugs . . . hell, I don't even take aspirin for my hangovers . . . but, my big brother has a major jones for anything he can snort or smoke, preferably snort. He's really into coke. So, I figure he'll probably use most of his to buy as much as he can suck up his nose."

There was a sad, but almost relieved, sound in her voice as she spoke, as if this was something she'd held in for a long time, and was finally letting it go.

"Ernie and I visited him yesterday," he said. "He didn't seem . . . I mean, I didn't notice any sign that he was using drugs."

Zelda laughed. It was a bitter sound.

"Oh, Garfield's what you call a high-functioning addict. He puts on a good show around strangers, kind of like an alcoholic who's learned to hide it from people."

Ed could relate to that. When he worked at the Pentagon, he'd had a colleague who seemed to be an okay, if indifferent, worker, and no one had even suspected that he was an alcoholic until they'd been on lockdown for six hours during a bomb threat, and he'd been unable to get to the bottle he kept stashed in his car in the parking lot. It was only when he was forced to be sober that his addiction had come to light. That probably explained the absence of other workers at his garage, Ed thought, or the lack of activity in the place.

"How does he manage to run a garage with a problem like that?"

"Like I said, he's high-functioning. I've seen him snort two lines of coke and then break down an engine and reassemble it. His addiction only shows when he can't get anything. When he's in withdrawal, believe me, like you don't want to be around him."

"Did your aunt know about this?"

"Uh, I don't know for sure. He like never used it around her, but Aunt Bea was pretty sharp, so it's possible she knew . . . why?"

A thought was beginning to form in Ed's mind, a thought he wasn't quite ready to share, not even with Ernie until he knew more.

"Oh, just asking. Do you have any idea where your aunt's copy of the new will might be?"

"No. When I . . . found her, that wasn't the

first thing on my mind, but after I calmed down . . . I looked around the living room and in her bedroom . . . I didn't find anything."

Given her distress at finding her aunt dead, Ed doubted very much that she'd done a good job of searching—unless she'd been somehow involved in the woman's death. He looked at her closely. No, he thought, I refuse to believe this woman, this child, as odd as she is, is capable of doing something so evil.

"Would you mind if we took another look?" he said. "Sometimes a new pair of eyes sees things that someone familiar with a place might overlook."

"No, I don't mind at all," she said without hesitation. "You want to go now?"

"Let's eat breakfast first," Rose said. "I do so hate working on an empty stomach."

"Good idea," Ed said. "First we eat, and then we go take another look around your aunt's place."

As they were walking toward the dining room, with Ed directly behind Zelda, she stopped so suddenly he bumped into her, brushing against her large posterior. His cheeks flamed and he jumped back as if he'd been burned.

"Sorry, I wasn't watching where I was going," he said.

Zelda turned, and smiled at him. "No problem. I stopped too fast. I just remembered one other thing I wanted to tell you."

"What?" Ed was thankful that she was not making an issue what part of his anatomy had made contact with what part of her anatomy. Even with the age difference, it had caused an automatic and, quite unwanted reaction.

"The county won't be able to do an autopsy on Aunt Bea."

"What reason did they give for refusing?"

"Oh, they didn't refuse, because I didn't ask them."

Ed's mouth dropped open. He frowned at her. "Have you changed your mind about her cause of death?"

"Oh no, I still don't think she died of a heart attack. I didn't ask for an autopsy because there's no longer a body to autopsy. When I called Garfield to talk to him about it, he informed me that he had Aunt Bea cremated yesterday morning. He said that's what she wanted, but she never told me she wanted to be cremated."

Charles Ray

Fourteen

They had a large breakfast of pancakes, hash browns, bacon, and scrambled eggs washed down with large glasses of orange juice and coffee. Violet had an irascible personality, but she was, Ed had do admit, one hell of a cook. He enjoyed the food, but his mind was on anything but food. He ate on autopilot.

Everyone else wanted to linger over a second cup—well, for Ed, Ernie, and Zelda, a third or fourth—of coffee, but Ed was anxious to get to Beatrice Terwilliger's house. Something wasn't right about this case, and he was determined to find out what.

"You guys go ahead and have more coffee if you want," he said. "I think that Zelda and I should go take a look through her aunt's house."

"Why don't you two take travel mugs," Rose said, rising from her place at the table and padding into the kitchen where she removed two silver mugs from the cabinet. After filling them, she returned to the dining room.

She handed them to Ed, who gave one to Zelda and tucked the other under his arm.

"Thanks," he said. He turned and headed for the living room with Zelda trailing closely behind. "Come on down and join us when you've finished your coffee," he said over his shoulder.

Outside the house, they turned right, and walked to the corner and then another right on Maple. They walked a block to the late Beatrice Terwilliger's small two-bedroom cottage, at the corner of Maple and Jonquil. PVC was just beginning to stir, or as much of a stir as could be expected from a community whose average age was well north of sixty. A few people were walking, or limping, some with the aid of shiny metal walkers and some with canes, toward the community center for breakfast. Ed recognized a few of them; familiar faces, but a few were strangers to him. As he walked, acknowledging the occasional greeting with a nod and a smile, he realized that in all the time he'd lived here, he'd never bothered to really get to know most of his neighbors. Except for Ernie and the Wertheim sisters, he hadn't bothered really to get to know anyone. Even most of the staff, except for Roland Vickers, Candice Drummond, and Janet Murphy, were just faces he vaguely noticed in passing. He wondered if Beatrice had gotten to know anyone in the community, or, like him, had just nodded absently at people without ever getting to know them. Would he, like her, die someday, and just be another excuse to attend a memorial service for someone you barely knew? The thought made him sad.

They crossed the street and walked up to the front door, where Zelda paused with her hand in her pocket and a tortured look on her face.

"It seems so strange going in here and knowing she won't be there," she said.

"I know it's hard for you, but if you want to know what really happened to your aunt, it's necessary."

She pulled a brass key from her pocket and held it an inch from the lock. "I know. I'm just so glad you're here, though. I don't think I could do this alone."

Ed didn't respond. After a few seconds, she sighed and plunged the key into the lock and turned. Slowly she pushed the door open and stood back, looking expectantly at Ed. He smiled and preceded her into the living room.

In size and configuration, it resembled his living room, but the furnishings were completely different. Where his furniture was plain and utilitarian, the furnishings in this room bordered on the ornate, and looked like they'd been transplanted from another era. An oversized couch covered in a twill-like light purple fabric with white lace doilies on the arms sat on the left. In front of it was a rectangular coffee table that looked like it had been carved from a single piece of dark walnut wood, and on the table were clones of the doilies, intricately crocheted white lace circles, one at each corner and a larger one in the center. Mismatched, but elegant looking chairs faced the sofa. One was a low, maroon recliner with footrest, and the other was a wooden chair with a high back and curved arms, made of some light colored wood. Photos and paintings of cats, dogs, and birds—mostly cats—adorned the walls. Lining the walls to either side of the doorway to the dining room were two long, low bookcases. Their tops and shelves were covered with knickknacks, little porcelain figurines and snow globes, all lined up precisely. Most of the figurines were of various species of domestic cat. Nothing really matched, but somehow, Ed thought, it seemed to work together, and it helped form a picture in his mind of the woman he didn't know, a woman who loved cats, but who had varied interests and tastes, which she combined in her own way into her life, like her living room.

Ed stood there for a moment, looking around to get a sense of the total space and layout. As he looked, he noticed the other difference between her place and his. In his, the closet was on the immediate left when you entered, but in hers it was a few feet further in and on the right.

"Okay, let's start in this room," he said. "Begin by describing exactly what you saw when you first opened the door."

Zelda came and stood beside him. She faced the entrance to the dining room and closed her eyes.

"I stepped inside, just as you and I did now, but for some reason I looked to the right, not the left," she said. Her voice sounded like she'd just awakened, but was not yet fully alert, sort of hollow like she was speaking from the bottom of a well. "Then I looked at the coffee table, and after that, the sofa. That's when I saw Aunt Bea lying there."

Ed placed a hand lightly on her shoulder.

"We'll need a bit more detail than that. For instance, when you opened the door and stepped inside, were the lights on?"

She opened her eyes, and then scrunched them almost shut. "Yeah, that's right. The lights were on. That's what caused me to look to the right first." She pointed to a pair of large gooseneck floor lamps, one behind each of the chairs facing the sofa. "Those two lamps were on, which was strange, because it was full light out and Aunt Bea never believed in using artificial light during the day."

Ed smiled. "Good, that's very good. See what I mean? Details like that are very important. Go on."

"Well, then I like looked over toward the sofa." She paused and closed her eyes again. "You want details right? First, I saw the coffee table. It had a teapot and a cup on it. First I saw the cup, and then the teapot. And then, I saw Aunt Bea stretched out on her side on the sofa. At first I thought she might be taking a nap, but then . . . I saw her eyes were open, and I . . . I knew—" Her eyes flooded with tears, and glistening rivulets streamed down her cheeks.

"Just relax," Ed said, feeling some of her pain as she recalled the incident. He had to get her mind back on the search. "You said you saw the cup and then the teapot. Which was closer to the sofa?"

She wiped the moisture from her cheeks, sniffled and turned her attention back to the coffee table. "Uh, it was the teapot. The teapot was closer to the sofa."

Ed tried to picture it in his own mind. The lamps on, the teapot, not the cup, closer to Beatrice; two inconsistencies, if Zelda's recollection was to be trusted, which he did. He didn't think she could fake the pain he was sensing.

"What did you do next?" he asked.

"Well, I called out to her." She blinked back tears. "I mean, like I knew she was dead from all the dead bodies I worked on in my job at the mortuary, but it just seemed the thing to do. I . . . I started over to check her pulse, and that's when I heard this like scratching sound from the closet over there. It was Petunia. Poor thing was frantic. I don't know how long she'd been in there, but it must've been a long time, because when I let her out, she ran straight to her litter box in the kitchen to relieve herself."

"You said before that the closet door was locked."

"Yeah. When I pulled on it, it didn't open. I checked and that little knob was turned all the way. I had to turn it to open the door."

"You don't think maybe your aunt did it, and forgot."

She shook her head vigorously. "No way. Aunt Bea would never do such a cruel thing. The only time she ever banished Petunia from the room was when Garfield came over. For some strange reason, he claims he's allergic to cats, but I think he just doesn't like them. Anyway, the few times he'd come over, Aunt Bea would put Petunia in the bedroom. I've never known her to put her in the closet, though."

Ed looked around the living room. There wasn't a piece of furniture with drawers, and nothing looking like a will was in evidence. He walked to the closet and pulled the door open. Inside there was a brown overcoat hanging on the rack, and a pair of rubber overshoes on the floor, but the closet was otherwise empty.

"I don't see anything of interest in here," he said. "Let's check the kitchen next. If I remember correctly, you said you took the teapot and empty cup in there?"

"Yeah, except the cup wasn't like empty. It was still full, and the teapot was half full. It was peppermint tea, one of Aunt Bea's favorites. I took them in and poured the tea down the sink and washed them both. Aunt Bea hated having dirty dishes around. I don't know, I guess just felt she'd have wanted me to clean things up."

He said nothing as he followed her through the dining room, bare but for an open face china cabinet, a dining table and four chairs, and more pictures of cats on the walls.

"Your aunt seems to have had a thing for cats," he said.

"Yeah, she did. She loved them. If the management here would have let her, she would've had a dozen living here with her."

Ed looked quickly into the china cabinet and under the table. Nothing. They went on into the kitchen, which was laid out similarly to his. The only wall adornment was a large round clock with a picture of a cat on the face. They stopped in front of the sink.

"Now, I want you to describe exactly what you saw that morning."

"I walked in and went directly to the sink," she said. "There was a cup on the drain board next to the sink . . . it matched the one that was in the living room. I poured the tea from the teapot and the cup, washed them, and left them upside down on the drain board like I always do when I help . . . helped Aunt Bea. Oh, I forgot to tell you, I called 911 just before I came to the kitchen, and I also called the switchboard, so they'd let the ambulance in. Anyway, after I washed the pot and cup, I went back to the living room and waited."

"So, you left everything upside down on the drain board?"

"Yeah . . . uh, no, not really. I remember now, the first cup was right side up."

"Could your aunt have left it like that?"

"I don't think so. She even put things like cups and glasses upside down in the cabinet. She said, it kept the dust out."

"Okay, let's check all the cabinets and drawers in here for that will, although, I don't think we'll find anything. I can't imagine your aunt keeping important papers in the kitchen."

They checked everywhere, including the garbage can, and found nothing. Next they checked both bedrooms, again coming up empty.

"I don't understand," Zelda said when they were back in the living room. "The lawyer said she took the revised will . . . that she wanted to study it and discuss it with me and Garfield, but it's nowhere to be found. How can that be?"

"That's a good question. The only answer that I can give you is that someone removed it. The question is, who?"

"Will you help me find out who did it?"

Not just who moved the will, Ed thought, but who was in the house with Beatrice Terwilliger. That was one thing he was sure of, but he wanted to discuss it with Ernie before deciding how to proceed.

"I'll do my best, Zelda," he said.

Fifteen

They'd done a thorough search of every room in the house by the time Ernie and the Wertheim sisters arrived to help, so everyone went back to their house. After lunch, Zelda left to rehearse with her band, and Ed and Ernie, after being told they wouldn't have to help with after-meal cleanup, went to Ed's house.

Ed opened a bottle of Scotch and put it, two glasses, a bowl of ice cubes, a legal pad and two pencils on the dining room table.

"So, I take it we're gonna do some strategizing, or is a better term brainstorming?" Ernie said.

"Brainstorming's probably a good term. We'll start with what we know and work from there to what we need to find out."

Ernie ripped off several sheets from the pad and took a pencil.

"For starters, we *know* that Bea be dead," he said. He wrote, *B. J. Dead* at the top of the top sheet.

Ed gave him a disapproving look.

"This is serious, Ernie. I mean, you're right, she's dead and that's the starting point, but we shouldn't make light of it."

"You believe Zelda about her not dying of a heart attack?" Ernie's face wrinkled in confusion.

"Yeah, and if you'll quit clowning around, I'll explain why."

Ed straightened the pad and picked up a pencil. At the top he wrote,

B. Terwilliger - Cause of Death unknown

Ernie's brows shot up. "Whoa! So you think Doc Vickers screwed up when he pronounced it a heart attack?"

"Quite possibly, although it's also possible that he looked at the body and honestly thought that's what it was. I think we need to have another talk with him. For now, though, let me show you why I think there's more to this than a simple heart attack. There are a few things that need explaining. Let me show you."

On the next line he wrote,

1. Lights on in the daytime

"There's nothing unusual about that," Ernie said.

"According to Zelda, her aunt never turned lights on during the daylight hours. I guess it was to save on her electricity bill. But, that's not the only thing."

2. The cat locked in the closet

He looked at what he'd written. "I know what you're thinking," he said. "But, I saw that closet, and the cat couldn't have locked himself in. I also saw the house. That woman was crazy about cats, you saw all the pictures. There's no way she would lock an animal in a closet like that. Then, there's this." He wrote,

3. Empty tea cup on kitchen counter
4. Tea cup in living room far from her

"I don't get it," Ernie said.

"Zelda said her aunt was fussy about cleaning and neatness. I saw that in the way she had everything on her shelves all lined up. It wouldn't be like her to leave a cup on the sink. And, if she was drinking tea, why was the teapot between her and the cup. It should have been the other way around."

"Wait a minute, are you saying there was someone else in the house?"

"That's exactly what I'm saying."

Any one of the items on Ed's list could be innocent—well, maybe not so innocent, he thought, but at least one of them alone would be weak. But, four things out of place like that in the house of a woman who had a place for everything, and a habit of putting everything in its place, they were a clear signal to Ed that something was amiss. The thought was hovering at the edge of his mind. He was reluctant to focus on it, because it was so horrible to contemplate.

"You think somebody might've killed the old lady?" Ernie asked.

There, Ed thought, it's been said. *If* someone else was in the house, and *if* Beatrice didn't die from a heart attack, it left the door wide open to someone assisting her into the hereafter.

"I don't know what to think, but there's one other strange item for my list." He wrote,

5. All copies of Bea's will missing

"Zelda and I looked all over that house," he said. "And, not only is the revised will missing, but we couldn't find the original.

Someone removed both, and that you have to agree, is a bit suspicious."

Ernie put the tip of his pencil to his lips and scrunched his eyes close for a few seconds. When he opened his eyes, he blinked as if surprised to find that he hadn't magically transported to some faraway place. Ed knew this was his way of thinking deeply on a subject.

"Yeah, I think you're right, it all sounds ve-e-e-ry suspicious, like maybe somebody done old Bea in. So, what do we do next?"

"Let's think about what we need to learn." Ed flipped the pad to a fresh sheet. "We already know we need to somehow determine cause of death," he said, writing, *Cause of Death*, at the top of the sheet.

"But, how're we gonna do that without a body?"

"I didn't say it'd be easy," Ed said. "We'll just have to intuit the cause of death from whatever evidence we find."

"Intuit, I like that word. It's what you do when you have no idea what the true answer is, right?"

Ed waggled his pencil at Ernie. "Scoff if you will," he said. "But, if we can get the answers to a few key questions, we just might be able to determine exactly how Beatrice died."

"Even without a body?"

"I didn't say it would be easy, but look at what we know already that indicates she wasn't alone at the time of her death."

"Like what?"

"Vickers said she'd been dead for several hours when he arrived, shortly after Zelda discovered the body. That, along with the lights being on, indicates she was in the living room late the night before. The cup on the sink and the cat being locked in the closet . . . oh, and the fact that the cup in the living room was on the wrong side of the table, tells me that there was someone else there."

He wrote, *Identify who was with her when she died,* on the second line.

"Okay, I see your point. If she had a visitor that night, we ought to be able to check with the gate and see who it was."

"The next thing we need to determine, assuming she didn't die of natural causes, is who would have a motive to kill her."

On the third line, he wrote, *Motive.*

Ernie nodded. "Money is the main reason people kill each other," he said.

"Which," Ed said, nodding in agreement. "Is why finding the revised copy of her will is so important, because I think that will give us a clue as to who has the greater motive."

On the fourth line, he wrote, *Where are the copies of the will?*

"You know, though, that means Zelda's a suspect. I mean, just 'cause she came to us and claimed her aunt didn't die of a heart attack, doesn't mean she didn't do anything wrong. She could just be doing that to misdirect us."

"That's always possible." Ed nodded. "But, my gut tells me she didn't do it."

"Then, that leaves her brother, Garfield."

"Kind of what I was thinking. Of course, we have one little problem."

"I know." Ernie's head went slowly up and down. "We have to be able to prove it, and we don't have a body or anyone who saw him here."

Ed ripped off the second sheet. "But we have our plan of attack," he said, holding it up,

Cause of Death
Identify who was with her
when she died
Motive
Where are the copies of the
will?

"Got 'em a little out of order, don't you?" Ernie asked.

"Yeah you're right; we need to find the will first. That'll help give us an idea who had a reason for killing her."

"You turned her house upside down and didn't find diddly. How do you plan to find it?"

"I'm still working on that one. In the meantime, I think we ought to have another chat with Vickers."

Sixteen

On the way to the administrative offices, Ed decided to take a detour, and swung by the main gate. The guard on duty, a heavyset, florid faced man with bright red hair and a gut that covered his belt buckle, greeted them with a smile.

"Mr. Lazenby, Mr. Cardoza, what can I do for you gentlemen today?" he asked as Ed and Ernie approached the kiosk in which he sat.

Ed was impressed that the man would know their names so easily, especially considering the fact that despite having seen him at the gate almost every day for several years, he had no idea what *his* name was.

Ed leaned slightly forward and looked at the name tag on the man's shirt. It read O'Meara. "Well, Officer O'Meara," he said. "I was wondering if you could explain the gate entry procedures to my friend here."

"Come on, Mr. Lazenby, you mean after all the years you've lived here, you don't know the rules for entering?"

"Well, I think I know, but Ernie here disagreed with me, so could you settle the argument. I say that everyone who comes in has to sign the logbook, but he disagrees. Everyone who comes in here does have to sign in, right?"

"Sure," O'Meara said. "They have to sign their name and give their destination, and then check out on the way out." He smiled, and then he snapped his finger. "Oh, there's one exception. Residents who have family members on the outside can register them, and all they have to do is show an ID when they drive in and out, and if they're on the list, they don't have to sign in."

Ed felt like he'd eaten food that was slightly off, a kind of hollowness in the pit of his stomach accompanied by the beginnings of an ache. "You mean, there's no record of relatives who come and go here?"

"Yup, that's the way it works. The residents insisted on it when the place first opened. Said they didn't want their relatives treated like terrorists or criminals or something. It makes sense, you know. We only have the check-in procedures in the first place to prevent crime and protect the people who live here, and their families are hardly a threat, right? Did I help you win the argument?"

"No, not really," Ed said. "But, it's good to know how things really work." But not so good to know that the procedures don't really protect us, he thought, as he nodded his thanks and walked away, with a frowning Ernie walking behind him.

"Well, that busts one lead all to hell and gone," Ernie said.

"All to hell and gone is right," Ed said. "There's no way we can prove Garfield was here Thursday night."

"Or Zelda either, for that matter," Ernie said. "I mean, there's no way to prove she *wasn't here*

Ed grimaced. "Or Zelda either." He was still *pretty* sure, deep in his gut that she wasn't guilty of anything but poor choice of careers and no fashion sense. "Well, let's go talk to Vickers. I have a few questions for him."

"You gonna question his diagnosis again?"

"No, I'm not even bringing Beatrice's case up this time. That's only make him defense. I have another idea that I think will play to Vickers' ego."

They continued walking toward the main building. When they were a few feet from the entrance, Ernie put a hand across Ed's chest. "You're not gonna tell me what your idea is?"

"Oh, just follow my lead when we get in," Ed said. "You're gonna love it. Besides, if I talk about it, it won't be as fresh, and I need it to sound that way when I bring it up to him. Don't worry, you're gonna like this."

Ernie made a sour face, but Ed just returned it with a placid, but determined look. After a few seconds, Ernie dropped the hand that was resting on Ed's chest. "Okay, we'll play it your way."

The lobby had a few more people than normal, mostly couples or small groups sitting around at the small tables having coffee or tea or reading. Two young women who looked like twins with coiled braids of blonde hair over their ears, looking like they'd started early preparing for Oktoberfest, stood behind the high reception desk smiling vacantly at everyone who passed near them. Ed and Ernie took a sharp right just before the desk and went through the door to the clinic and administrative wing. The clinic was empty, even Nurse Drummond was off somewhere, probably treating a sprained ankle in one of the many gardens that dotted the community.

Lydia Myers sat at her desk, now reading a magazine with a picture of a skinny fashion model on the cover instead of studying her nails. She was still chewing gum. She looked up as they entered. Her eyes went wide when she recognized, and the motion of her jaw stopped with her mouth agape. They beamed broad smiles at her.

"Don't tell me," she said without enthusiasm. "You're here to see Dr. Vickers again, and you don't have an appointment."

"Well, if you insist, I won't tell you, but it will make it difficult for us to see him, don't you think?" Ernie said.

"Huh?

"Don't play with her like that, Ernie," Ed said. "Of course we'd like to see Dr. Vickers, and we'll only need a few minutes of his time."

She began chewing her gum, her eyes half closed in concentration. Finally, her face relaxed, and she stopped chewing.

"Go right on in," she said, and turned her attention back to her magazine.

Ed and Ernie smiled at each other and moved quickly to the door to Vickers' office and eased it open. They entered quietly, but could have saved the effort. Vickers was behind his desk, leaned back in his chair with his mouth half open, snoring softly. Ernie shut the door with a bang. Vickers' eyes popped open and he shot upright in his chair, scooting it backwards until it banged into the wall.

"Uh, ooh, wha—". He rubbed at his eyes. "Edward, Ernesto, what are you doing here? Is there a problem?" Pulling himself back to his desk, he brushed at imaginary lint on his sleeves.

Holding back his own laugh, Ed elbowed Ernie in the side when he chuckled. "No, doc," he said. "Look, sorry to bother you. I know you're busy and all, but I need a little advice, and I think you're the only person who can help me."

Vickers sat straighter and puffed out his chest.

"Well, of course, you know I'm always available for the residents of this community. Please have a seat." He waved at the two chairs flanking his desk. "What is it that you want to know?"

Ed sat and folded his hands on his lap. "You know how you're always encouraging residents to find constructive outlets for their energies and creative pursuits to keep out minds active." Ed remembered no such advice from Vickers, but he knew that the man so craved public approval he wouldn't think about whether or not he'd ever said such a thing.

"Of course," Vickers said, gushing. "A healthy mind and body are essential to long life and good health."

I wonder what cereal box he read that from, Ed wondered, but kept his expression impassive. "Well, I've decided to take up writing," he said. "I'm writing a mystery novel, and I need your help with some technical stuff."

Leaning back in his chair with a self-satisfied look on his face, Vickers lifted his hands in a tent-shape with his fingertips touching his bottom lip.

"That's very interesting. I think a creative pursuit like that is a wonderful idea. You know, I've often toyed with the idea of writing a book, if I only had the time. A mystery, eh? Let me guess; you want to know all the ways you could kill someone so that it wouldn't be detected—the perfect murder, right?"

Ed smiled. This will be even easier than I planned, he thought. "That's absolutely right," he said. "I want my hero to find a body, and it looks like the victim died of natural causes, but in reality was murdered. But, I have no idea how such a crime could be committed."

Vickers half closed his eyes, lost in thought. Then, he smiled, a wolfish grin that caused Ed to shudder.

"Well, you've come to the right place," Vickers said. "No one's better qualified to discuss causes of death than a physician. If you wanted to kill someone and not have it look like murder, there are some substances that will do the trick; some poison plants, for instance, like oleander, monkshood, lily of the valley, and belladonna. Then, you have some medicines like codeine, oxycodone, or Quaaludes, and drugs like cocaine or phencyclidine. All are extremely toxic, kill quickly with the right dosage, and most bodies don't look like they've been assaulted."

"You mean, they look like the person died of natural causes?"

"Many of them do. Some cause vomiting or contortion of facial features, but some just cause the heart to stop, and the person dies relatively quickly and painlessly. Unless foul play is suspected and there's an autopsy, it would look just like a heart attack, and even when an autopsy's done, unless the specific element is tested for, it might still be missed and the death ruled a heart attack."

"Good grief," Ed said. "I'm not sure I want you writing me a prescription, especially not if you're upset with me."

"Oh, I'm a strict follower of the Hippocratic Oath. I would never intentionally harm a patient. I just remember a lot of this stuff from med school. After all, if you're going to treat people who're ill, you need to know about the things that make them ill. There are so many things around us every day, insecticides, household and industrial chemicals . . . even some garden plants, that can harm us, a doctor has to be aware of them." He stopped talking for a second and stared dreamily at the ceiling, than he opened his eyes and continued talking. He had a goofy looking smile on his face, an expression Ed had never seen on the man's face before. "There was this one classmate of mine, Cynthia Barker, who was fascinated with poisons. I picked up a lot of what I know about them from her. You would be amazed at how many things we think are harmless are actually toxic, like peach pits, for instance. Of course, the ones I mentioned to you would be the ones that would be most effective in a mystery story, don't you think.

What's your story about, by the way?"

"It's about this . . . old guy who lives by himself. He has a lot of money and only a couple of relatives to inherit it. The thing is, they get tired of waiting for him to die, so one of them—or maybe both of them, I haven't decided that part yet—decide to help him along. Of course, they have to make it look natural, or they can't inherit. You've given me some good ideas to work on, and I really appreciate it." He stood, and motioned Ernie to do the same. "I think I've taken up too much of your time. Ernie and I'll be going."

Vickers looked disappointed. "Don't you want some more details to make it realistic?"

"More details?"

"Of course, like the best method of administering the substance, how much you should use, how long it takes to work, things like that. I imagine some of your readers would appreciate the verisimilitude, for instance, if you want the victim to die without a lot of mess, you could use something like phencyclidine. It doesn't cause the victim to vomit like many of the other poisons do, and the right dose is pretty lethal and fast. You'd have a corpse that looked exactly like it had a heart attack, which in fact is what it would be."

"That's the second time you've mentioned this phencycli-, thing. What is it, and how would the average person get hold of it?"

"Oh, sorry . . . phencyclidine, or more

commonly known by its street name, PCP, is a strong tranquilizer. It's no longer legal for use in humans, but some vets still use it for large animals. It was quite popular with addicts in the 1970s, but less so now, although I understand it's still available. It removes inhibitions, gives the users incredible strength, and makes them impervious to pain. The problem is, children, the ill, or the elderly can have a very severe reaction to it, and by severe, I mean their hearts can stop. If an old person were administered a fatal dose of PCP, say in food or drink, they could go into cardiac arrest in less than twenty minutes. There'd be no vomit or other signs of anything other than a heart attack. If no autopsy was performed, it would be the perfect crime."

"What would be a fatal dose?"

"That's hard to say. It would depend upon the health of the victim, and, of course, body weight."

"Wow," Ernie said. "You doctors know some scary stuff. You could literally get away with murder."

Vickers stared at Ernie, his brow wrinkled. "Unfortunately, there have been doctors, a very, very few, mind you, who have been so psychopathic they've used their medical knowledge to kill. But, believe me, such cases are rare. We're trained to use our knowledge to help people, and you have to admit, if a mystery writer wanted information about the terrible things that can be done to the human body, there's no better source of information than a doctor."

That kind of information, Ed realized, would be useful, but only if he had some idea which substance was used, or how it might have been introduced into Beatrice Terwilliger's body. It was getting late in the day, though, and he had one more thing he wanted to do before the day ended, and that didn't include sitting in Vickers' office listening to the man drone on, no matter how useful his information was.

"That's a good idea. I tell you what; I'm still trying to figure out how I want to stage that particular scene. That'll sort of determine what kind of poison might be appropriate, don't you think. Once I have that worked out, would it be okay if I came back and talked to you again?"

"Why, of course, and I'd be more than happy to read your final manuscript to check for accuracy, if you'd like." There was a hopeful look on Vickers' face.

"Shucks, I really would appreciate that," Ed said. "I'll have to do a special dedication section just to thank you for all your help."

Vickers looked at Ed, beaming a smile that threatened to stretch his face out of shape.

"I look forward to seeing what you've written."

On their way out, Ed had to elbow Ernie

to keep him from laughing. Not that Vickers, sitting there looking up at the ceiling with a dreamy expression on his face would have noticed. He never even made the connection with Beatrice, Ed thought. Good God, I hope I never get sick in this place.

Seventeen

As they walked to Ed's house, he explained to Ernie what he wanted to do before supper. They had the usual argument over which vehicle to take, and again Ed prevailed, so they headed out in his 4-Runner, a sullen Ernie hunched against the door on the passenger side with his arms across his chest.

It took them ten minutes to get to Garfield's Garage, thanks to the lack of west and southbound traffic, and for once Ed encountered no hostile, road-hogging drivers to set his teeth on edge and make him consider shredding his driver's license and donating his vehicle to Goodwill.

Ed pulled into the littered parking lot, and this time ignored the hulks scattered around, parking near the building, next to a powder blue Lincoln Continental that looked brand new except for a few scratches on the left rear quarter panel.

The large repair bay looked much as it had on their first visit, but near the corner that held the small office, they saw three figures standing close together. It was clear, though, that they weren't a threesome—more a duo hovering, or looming over a third person, and that third person was Garfield Terwilliger. Still dressed in his coveralls, he stood with his back to the office wall, hunched with his hands held up in a posture of supplication and a look of fear on his ashen face.

As Ed neared, and got a closer look at the duo, he wasn't sure which one of them inspired the greater fear in the cowering man. One was big—in fact, big was an inadequate description—with what looked like muscles overlaying muscles like piles of rope, shoulders a yard wide that tapered down to a narrow waist and then flared back out slightly into muscled legs that strained against the dark pants he wore. His hands were as large as small hams, with prominent knuckles, and he kept clenching and unclenching them as if he wanted to hit something—that something being, obviously, Garfield. The other man was small. Narrow, stooped shoulders and a sunken chest over a slight paunch, which was the only thing holding his light gray pants up. He had slender hands with manicured nails. His face could only be described as . . . narrow; a thin, pointed nose over thin lips, cat-like eyes, and tiny ears, all set in an egg-shaped head covered with thin brown hair that was slicked down on his skull. He looked like a rat that had transformed into a man, but only partially. The eyes, Ed thought, were like the eyes of a snake, cold and unblinking. He had the kind of look that gave you chills and made you want to turn and go back the way you came.

Upon reflection, he decided that the smaller man was probably the most dangerous of the two, and was the one in charge, and as he neared the trio, the man spoke, confirming his assessment.

"Listen, dude," he said in a voice devoid of all emotion. "You better not be blowing smoke, 'cause the boss won't like that, and if the boss is unhappy, well then, me and Moose here will be unhappy. You get my drift?"

"S-sure, Turk," Terwilliger said. "I s-swear, I ain't blowin' smoke. It's all gonna be cool, I promise. Just give me a few days, okay?"

"Lemme do 'im just a little anyway, Turk," the big man said in a surprisingly mild, almost childlike voice. "Just so he knows we ain't jokin'."

Terwilliger tried to melt into the wall behind him, his hands thrown up in front of his face.

"No-o-o-o, please, guys don't. I promise I'll come up with it."

The smaller man, turning to look up at his companion, saw Ed and Ernie. His small eyes got smaller, closing almost to slits. He put a hand on the big man's arm.

"Take it easy, Moose. I think he got the message. If it turns out he din't . . . well, we'll come back and you can have your fun," he then turned and shot his laser-like gaze at Ed and Ernie, and said, "Who the fuck are you old dudes?"

"We're friends of Garfield's sister," Ed said. "Who are you?" He locked eyes with the little man, keeping his gaze level.

The little man, Turk, looked from Ed to Terwilliger with a wolfish smile on his face. "Hey, looks like that Goth sister of yours has decided to branch out and try some old dark meat, dude." He turned back to Ed. "What you doing here, pops?"

He knew that it was foolish, but Ed didn't particularly like having some young punk talking down to him. "That's between us and Garfield," he said. "Family business, you understand." He stared coldly down at the skinny little guy, despite the fact that he felt like he had a block of ice in his belly. He had no doubt the little weasel had a weapon and wouldn't hesitate to use it if pushed too far.

The little man looked at him, scowling for several heartbeats. Then, he cocked his head back and laughed. "I like you, old dude," he said between chuckles. "You got you some spunk. I guess I can see what the Goth chick sees in you." He turned back to Terwilliger. "Look, dude, we're leavin' now, but don't you forget what I told you. Let's go, Moose."

Without waiting for the big man to answer, the little man brushed past Ed and walked toward the entrance. The big man, Moose, stood there a few seconds, looking confused.

"I *said*, come on, Moose," the little man said over his shoulder. "That means *now!*"

"Yeah, okay, Turk, I'm comin'," the big man said, blinking rapidly. He, too, brushed past Ed, bumping him as he did, and rushed to catch up with the little man, who was clearly the alpha of their little pack.

After the two of them were out the door, and Ed heard the throaty sound of the Lincoln's eight cylinder engine, he turned to face Terwilliger.

"Who were your friends, Garfield?" he asked.

Still pale and shaking, Terwilliger looked blankly at Ed, quickly blinking his eyes like a man who'd been suddenly roused from a deep sleep.

"T-they're not m-my friends," he said. "They j-just work for a g-guy I do b-business with."

"What kind of business?"

Terwilliger shook himself. His eyes grew wide, and then narrowed to tiny slits. "That's none of your b-business. What are you d-doing here?"

Ed fixed him with a steely gaze. "Garfield, we need to talk."

"We got nothing to talk about. Leave me alone."

Still shrinking back against the door, he wiped a sleeved arm across his nose and sniffed. Ed sniffed too, but not from a runny nose; the odor coming from Garfield Terwilliger was enough to make Ed's eyes water. It smelled like he hadn't bathed in days.

"Actually," Ed said. "I think we do." He held his breath and crowded in close, leaving no room for Terwilliger to move. "Why don't we go into your office?"

Terwilliger pushed away from the wall and glared up at Ed. His lips quivered as he spoke. "I told you before, leave me alone. You got no business poking your noses into my business."

Despite the odiferous stench from his mouth as he spoke, that threatened to overwhelm Ed, he stood his ground, and returned Terwilliger's glare, dart for dart.

"Your sister, Zelda, asked for our help," he said. At the mention of his sister's name, Terwilliger flinched.

"You can't pay any attention to what Zelda says," he said, his lips still quivering. "You know she used to work in a funeral parlor, putting makeup on stiffs, right? Did she tell you why she had to quit?"

"No, but I have a feeling you're about to."

"Before I do, lemme ask you a question . . . did she say Aunt Bea didn't die of a heart attack?"

Ed's brows twitched. Terwilliger smiled and nodded.

"I'll take that as a yes," he said. "Now, I'll tell you why she had to stop working with dead people. She thought they were talking to her, telling her how they died. She got so freaky, nobody at the mortuary wanted to even be in the same room with her. They finally asked her to leave."

Ed breathed in and out slowly and tried to control the shock he felt at hearing that piece of information. He still believed that there was more to Beatrice's death than appearances seemed to indicate, but if Zelda was subject to 'hearing' the voices of the dead, it would complicate the hell out of any effort to get someone in authority to look into the case.

When he could trust his voice, he said, "So, you think your aunt died from a heart attack?"

"That's what that doctor . . . Vickers . . . that's what he said."

"That wasn't my question. Do *you* think she had a heart attack? Did she have a history of heart problems?"

"I don't know, maybe . . . hell, don't all old people have heart problems?"

Sweat had popped out on his upper lip, and a muscle in his left cheek was twitching like crazy. He studied the floor at Ed's feet.

"No, Garfield," Ed said. "All old people do not have heart problems, and I have a sneaking suspicion that your aunt was one of those people. When's the last time you saw her?"

"The last time I saw her?"

Ed's antenna slid up. It'd been a long time since he'd taken that course in counterintelligence, but he remembered some of the clues the instructor had said should be looked for to indicate when a subject was telling a lie, and repeating the question and avoiding eye contact were both high on the list.

"Yes, the last time you saw her, how long ago was it?"

"Uh, I don't remember, maybe two, three weeks . . . maybe even a month."

"And yet, you're the one who has to take care of all the arrangements now that she's dead. Why is that?"

"Hey, like I told you, my kid sister's a bit of a flake. As the older one, it's my responsibility. Anyway, what business is it of yours?"

Some of his truculence was coming back, but he still wouldn't look Ed in the eye.

"I just have one more question and I'll leave you alone," Ed said.

"I ain't promising to answer, but if it'll get you out of my face, go ahead."

"When we were here the other day, why

didn't you tell us you'd already cremated your aunt's remains?"

Mouth agape, Garfield Terwilliger now made brief eye contact with Ed, then darted his gaze away. "Uh, that's none of your business really," he said. "But, Aunt Bea wanted it that way. Now, I answered your question, so go on and get out of my garage. I have work to do."

Ed wanted to ask more questions, lots more questions. He knew he was being fed a line of bull. But, he also knew that a direct confrontation would likely yield nothing, and it would alert Terwilliger to his suspicions. No, he thought, he would have to be cagey and go at this case indirectly.

First, though, he needed to talk to Zelda.

Charles Ray

Eighteen

Ed dropped Ernie off in front of his house and then drove into his garage. Inside the kitchen, he called Violet Wertheim to get Zelda's phone number. Zelda answered on the second ring.

"Hello, Zelda here, how can I help you?" Her voice sounded chipper in his ear.

"Zelda, this is Ed Lazenby. I . . . uh, I need to ask you a question that's kind of personal and sensitive, but I really need you to give me a straight answer."

"Sure thing, Ed, anything you want to know."

He hesitated. A part of him didn't want to ask the question because he didn't want to know the answer. But, another part, that part that could never resist a mystery, that had to solve every unsolved puzzle, was driven to know. For two seconds the two halves wrestled with each other, and finally, the curious half of his nature won out.

"Why did you really stop working in the

mortuary?"

She laughed. "Like I told you when we first met, I wanted to be a musician," she said. He felt a twinge of disappointment, but before he could press her on it, she continued speaking. "But, that wasn't the whole story. There was another reason that I didn't mention because I guess I like thought you might think I was batty if you knew."

"I do think you're a very unusual young lady, but I *don't* think you're batty, not in the least."

"Hah, is that so? Okay, let me tell you why I quit working with dead people, and tell me if you still think I'm not cuckoo. The work was okay for the first few years, a little boring, but not too bad. At least I never got any customer complaints—at least, not the ones I worked on." She laughed. Ed remained silent, unsure if laughter on his part would be appropriate. "But, after a while, maybe it was from working alone in the basement of the funeral parlor, just me and the dead, I started hearing voices in my head. It was like they were speaking to me, you know, like telling me how they died, what they missed doing in their lives, things like that. At first, I didn't pay it any attention, but it kept happening. Like the naïve idiot I was, I mentioned it to my boss, the director of the place. He just told me I was working too hard, and gave me a few days off, but when I came back, the voices came back too. I guess I must've creeped the other people working there out, because after a month, my boss *suggested* that I might be better off in another line of work. Tell you the truth, I was starting to creep myself out." She paused a few seconds. "Anyway, I'd always wanted to be a musician . . . I played drums in a group in high school, so I left my job in the mortuary makeup business and after a week or so, I found this band whose drummer had just taken off, and the rest is history. So, you still think my elevator goes to the top floor?"

He would have loved to be able to see her face and body language to be sure, but the tone of her voice, and the fact that she hadn't tried to deny or sugarcoat anything was convincing. He was pretty sure that his first impression of her had been correct.

"All the way to the penthouse, young lady," he said. "All the way to the penthouse."

"So, anything new on what really happened to Aunt Bea?"

There was and there wasn't. He had his suspicions, but lacked a shred of hard proof, so it wasn't the time to share his thoughts with her. The truth, though, was buried somewhere under a mound of information and little hints, none of which made any sense at the moment.

He would just have to keep digging.

"Nothing yet, but I'm just getting started," he said.

Charles Ray

Nineteen

There was something about Wednesdays that had always affected Ed strangely, something that had never made any sense, but was no less profound in its impact on him. In that regard, he thought, he wasn't all that different from Zelda and her 'voices' of the dead.

On Wednesdays, the middle of the week, or hump day to the thousands of mindless drones he'd traveled with back and forth to his desk job at the Pentagon until he finally decided he'd had enough and had put in his request for retirement, he always felt a bit depressed. The week, he realized, was half over, and he'd not done half the things he ought to have done. Wednesday became for him a metaphor for life in many ways—it reminded him of all the things he'd yet to do, or had left undone or only partly done. So, unlike his colleagues who saw hump day as a day to rejoice that the week was half over, that much closer to goof-off time, he saw it as a day to lament the work not done. Where most people bitched about their Blue Mondays, Ed silently suffered his Woeful Wednesdays.

This particular Wednesday was no different. He woke up thinking about the task he'd taken upon himself, and the fact that, while he'd piled up lots of facts, he'd yet to see the problem clearly, and had, thusly, achieved nothing.

A hot shower did nothing to improve his mood. He brooded as he brushed his teeth and shaved. He ran the situation over in his mind as he dressed in dark brown slacks and a tan shirt. He mumbled to himself as he slipped his feet first into brown and black argyle socks and then into a brown pair of leather loafers.

After getting dressed, he sat on the edge of his bed, contemplating calling Ernie and walking with him to breakfast at the community center, but then decided that he was, in his current gloomy mood, not a fit meal companion, so he rose and padded toward the kitchen. "Nothing like a cup of fresh brewed coffee and an overdose of carbs to lighten a gloomy mood," he said to himself.

It wasn't lost on him that he'd spoken aloud. "Now, I'm talking to myself."

The first thing he did upon arrival in the kitchen was get a pot of coffee brewing. Next, he took six slices of bacon from the crisper in his fridge, arranged them on a paper towel he'd spread on a large plate, and then covered them with another piece of paper towel. He put this in the microwave and set if for four minutes. Quickly, the smell of bacon and brewing coffee filled the room.

"Now, I wonder what'd go good with that?" He smiled at the specter of himself talking to the wall. "Biscuits, hashed browns, and scrambled eggs, that's what."

His mind made up, and with clear goals in mind, he felt an immediate improvement in his mood. He found that when he was busy, no matter what it was that kept him busy, he had no time for negative thoughts.

As he set his oven to 325 degrees, the microwave dinged. He took the plate out and removed the top paper towel. He set the plate on the counter to allow the bottom towel to absorb the grease, which would leave the bacon nice and crisp. Then, he turned his attention to one of his specialties; buttermilk biscuits like his grandmother had taught him how to make when he was barely tall enough to see over the edge of the big wooden table in the center of her kitchen. Into a big mixing bowl, he dumped two cups of flour, a teaspoon of salt, and a teaspoon of baking powder, mixing them well. He then cut in two tablespoons of vegetable oil—his grandmother always used lard, but his years of listening to army doctors talk about the dangers of saturated fat had weaned him off solid fats, and truth be told, the taste was about the same. He poured buttermilk in, mixing all the while, until he had a dough that was tacky and wet, but still held together, which he dumped onto a floured cutting board and kneaded it, forming a quarter-inch-thick semi-circle. He dipped a water glass in the flour container, coating the rim, and then used it to stamp out a dozen 3-inch diameter biscuits which he arranged on a pizza pan. After smearing the tops of each with buttermilk, he put the pan in the oven, and turned his attention to the potatoes, which was a simple matter of peeling, shredding, mixing with shredded onion, salt, garlic powder, black pepper, and enough flour to enable him to make six little round patties. These went into a black iron skillet whose bottom had been coated with the same oil he used in the biscuits and put on the stove on medium high heat. They immediately began to sizzle. A peek through the glass door of his oven showed him that the biscuits had risen nicely and were golden brown on top, so he removed them and set them on the counter next to the bacon. The final step was preparing scrambled eggs. Most people just broke the eggs into a bowl, added salt and pepper and whipped them before cooking. That, however, wasn't the way Ed had been taught to do scrambled eggs. He broke six eggs into another mixing bowl, added salt, pepper, and garlic powder before whipping them into a frothy mixture. To this he added chopped green onions, chopped jalapeno peppers, a handful of diced tomatoes, two tablespoons of shredded parmesan cheese, and a quarter cup of buttermilk. After turning the potatoes and browning them nicely on both sides, he slid them onto a platter and poured the whipped egg mixture into the skillet, stirring it with a spatula until he had a soft yellow mound of scrambled eggs that slipped easily out of the skillet when he tipped it over a plate.

When he was done, he looked at the food spread out on the counter and realized that he'd cooked far more than he could eat alone, so he decided he might as well invite Ernie to join him. Just as he reached for the phone on the wall near the counter, it rang, startling him.

"Hello," he said.

"Is this the Lazenby residence?" Ed recognized the gruff tone of Carl Janzen's voice.

"Yeah, Carl it is, what can I do for you?"

"Do you know a gentleman by the name of Garfield Terwilliger by any chance?"

Ed detected a tension in his voice. This wasn't a social call, and it wasn't about a pleasant subject.

"I wouldn't exactly call young Mr. Terwilliger a gentleman, but I am acquainted with him. Why do you ask?"

Janzen cleared his throat. "You've been to his place of business?"

"Yes, twice in fact, but you still haven't answered my question . . . what's this about?"

"Look Ed, I know you and Ernie get bored over there at the retirement home, and you like to play detective, but sometimes you can take it too far."

"First of all, Carl, it's a retirement community, not a home," Ed said stiffly. "And, we are . . . I am *not* bored."

"But, you two have been playing detective . . . say, I just made the connection. You called me about a woman in your community who died, and now I remember . . . her name was Terwilliger. Is this guy Garfield Terwilliger related?"

"Yes, he's her nephew. Zelda, the young woman I mentioned on the phone is his sister."

"She's the one who thinks her aunt didn't die of a heart attack?"

"That's right," Ed said. "And, I'm inclined to believe her."

"Based on what hard evidence?"

That, Ed thought wryly, was the rub. He had no hard evidence.

"Just a gut feeling at the moment, nothing

I could bring to you.

"Ahem, well that's why I called, Ed. Without hard evidence, you can't go around accusing people of something, you know."

"What? I haven't— . . . did Garfield Terwilliger tell you that I accused him of something?"

"Yeah, he said you came to his garage and accused him of killing his aunt. Now, Ed, that's pretty serious. Not exactly criminal, but he could sue you for defamation."

Ed's cheeks felt hot. "Carl, I assure you that I did no such thing. I did ask him if he was aware of any heart problems his aunt had, but I never even hinted that I thought he might have hurt her."

Long pause. The only sound was Janzen clearing his throat. "Okay, I believe you," he said. "Maybe he just misunderstood you. But, just to be on the safe side, maybe you ought to stay away from him and his place."

"Did he file an official complaint?" Ed asked.

"No, I told him there was nothing to support a criminal complaint, and didn't say anything about a civil suit, but he was pretty hot under the collar, so remember what I said, stay away from him."

"Of course . . . if I'd known he was so sensitive I wouldn't have gone to his place the first time."

"Good. Now you and that pal of yours try to stay out of trouble." Janzen broke the connection before Ed could respond.

Ed hung the phone up. He felt a twinge of guilt for having lied to Janzen. The man was a good guy and a decent cop, but Ed had no intention of letting up on Garfield Terwilliger, no bloody way in hell. He snatched the phone up and dialed Ernie's number.

"Ernie," he said when his friend answered. "I just cooked enough to feed a platoon. Come over and help me eat it. We've got some planning to do."

Twenty

Over breakfast, Ed told Ernie of Janzen's call and outlined his planned action.

"But, didn't Carl tell us not to stick our noses into police business?" Ernie asked.

"Yeah, he did."

"So, why are you thinking about doing it?"

"Hey, he said don't go back to the garage," Ed said. "I don't plan to do that. What we have to do can mostly be done right here in PVC. We only have to pay one more short visit."

Despite the logic—Ed felt that his plan was perfectly logical—it still took until lunch to convince Ernie to go along with it. Like Ed, Ernie liked and respected Janzen, and was reluctant to do something that the detective had explicitly told them not to do. But, Ed was adamant and persistent, and he constantly reminded Ernie that Janzen had only told him that they shouldn't go back to Terwilliger's garage and confront the man, and confronting him wasn't part of his plan, so by mid-afternoon and their fifth cup of coffee, Ernie finally gave in—but only on the condition that they use his pickup rather than Ed's 4-Runner, arguing that since they'd already been to the garage twice in Ed's car, it might be unwise to drive it there again. As much as he disliked pickups, Ed had to agree that it made sense, and, if it got Ernie's agreement to go along it was a small sacrifice, so he agreed.

At ten past midnight, Ed put on a pair of dark blue slacks and a black shirt, and met Ernie in his garage. Ernie was dressed similarly, and any of the doubts he'd had earlier seemed to have dissipated at the prospect of having an adventure. At 12:20, with Ernie driving just below the speed limit so as not to attract attention, they left PVC and headed south. Traffic was almost nonexistent except for a few night owls or graveyard shift workers. They didn't encounter the usual mindless drivers who lane changed without signaling, tailgated, or whipped around you only to cut back in immediately in front of you and put on their brake lights—something about a pickup, Ernie often said, that discouraged such behavior. Despite this, Ernie kept a light foot on the gas pedal, so it was 12:45 when they neared the fenced-in area around Garfield's

Garage.

"I don't think it'd be a good idea to pull in there," Ed said, as Ernie slowed.

"Uh, oh yeah, guess you're right." Ernie picked up speed and drove past the gate.

Two blocks beyond they found an all-night convenience store/gas station with a nearly empty parking lot. Ernie pulled in and parked at the corner of the building near an ice machine. They looked around as they got out. There were two other cars in the lot, both empty. Through the oil-grimed plate glass window they could see the bored night clerk dozing behind the counter near the cash register.

"I'd suggest buying something so no one complains about us parking here," Ed said. "But, I think that guy would complain that we interrupted his nap. Let's go."

They made their way to the sidewalk and walked the two blocks back to Garfield's Garage. As they approached the gate, Ed stopped and held a hand up to stop Ernie. Through the fence he could see the dark hulks of the wrecks scattered about the lot around the big metal building. The big sliding door, down now, was a dark rectangle against the dark gray metal of the building. To the left of the door he saw two blurred orange rectangles about six feet apart and four feet above ground level. He hadn't noticed the windows on his previous visits.

"Looks like there might be someone

working late," he said. "We need to move in cautiously. It wouldn't do to be seen, especially right after being told to stay away."

Ernie nodded his agreement. "I wonder why anyone would be working so late at night."

Ed was wondering the same thing. "Let's go take a look and find out," he said.

The gate was hanging ajar. That probably made sense, Ed thought. There wasn't anything around the place that looked worth stealing. There was just enough space for him and Ernie to slip through. With Ernie close on his heels, he made his way slowly past the silent hulks, keeping to the deep shadows, and angling for the left side of the building.

They made it to the corner and moved up against the metal wall, crouching low. Up against the building, they could hear the hum of a generator and the crack and sizzle of what he assumed was an acetylene torch. Ed signaled for Ernie to be quiet and began crab walking toward the nearest window. When they reached the window, the sounds from inside became louder, and he noticed that the orange glow from the window flickered, confirming his guess that a torch was being used.

"I'm going to try and peek through the window and see if I can see what's going on inside," he whispered to Ernie. "Keep a lookout so nobody can sneak up on us."

Ed could hear the creaking of Ernie's knees as he crab walked past to the other side of the window, and when he stood slowly, rubbing his knees and wincing as he did so. The sight and sounds of his friend's discomfort made him aware of a slight twinge in his right knee from kneeling beneath the window so long. Maybe, he thought, we're too old for this kind of nonsense. No, he chided himself silently, we just need to exercise more. He still moved slower than usual, though, as he braced against the wall to stand. He ignored the tiny stab of pain in his knees and eased around until the right side of his head was in front of the window.

Smeared with who knows how many months—or years—of grease, the glass did not offer a totally clear view. The images he saw were barely recognizable as people until he moved his head so that he could look with both eyes, and then it was like looking into one of those distorting mirrors at a circus.

He saw a figure dressed in coveralls, with a welding face shield on—he assumed that was Terwilliger—and kneeling beside a dark, car-shaped object, with a bright spear of light—the torch—sticking out in front. Behind the kneeling figure, he could make out two others, one small and one extremely large—Terwilliger's earlier visitors, perhaps—standing next to or leaning against a long, grayish object with silver stripes. Sparks flew from the bright spear of light when the kneeling figure brought it near the car shape. Through the greasy glass, Ed couldn't tell if something was being cut away or welded on the dark vehicle. What was obvious, though, was that he and Ernie wouldn't be able to 'inspect' the place. He pulled away from the window, and motioned for Ernie to follow him back to the corner of the building. Just before ducking to pass the window, Ernie took a quick peek through the glass. His brows arched upwards and his eyes went wide. He opened his mouth to speak, but Ed motioned him to silence. He couldn't be sure, that close to the window, that the noise of the generator and torch would cover their voices. He'd read somewhere that glass vibrated when sound struck it, so he worried that this might expose them to the three men inside the garage. He waited until they were back at the corner of the building before speaking.

"I didn't expect to find anyone here at this hour," he whispered. "Guess we won't be able to . . . take a look inside."

"Yeah, and considering what they're doing, it might be a good idea for us to get the hell out of here," Ernie said.

"Whaddaya mean what they're doing?"

"Aw hell, I forgot, you spent all that time workin' in the Pentagon, you don't know what goes on out here in the real world. Ed, my man, this here's a chop shop operation."

"Chop . . . you mean—"

"Exactamundo, my friend," Ernie said.

"They're cutting stolen cars up and peddling the parts. That's why they're workin' so late."

"I guess that also explains why there was no one around during the day."

"Uh, right, that's what I just said. Now, let's get the hell out of here before they spot us. Some of these hot car operations can be pretty rough."

"You think they'd beat us up or something if they caught us peeking in on them?"

"Yeah, if we were lucky."

"And, if we were unlucky?"

"You don't want to know."

They made their way quietly, but at a faster pace than when they'd come in, back to the gate, and didn't stop walking until they were back at the convenience store.

After making sure they weren't being followed, they made their way to Ernie's truck and got in.

"Well, this certainly puts a new wrinkle on things," Ed said. "Not only is young Garfield a drug addict, but he's involved in a car theft ring."

"What are we gonna do about it?"

Ed was silent for several seconds, thinking about what they now knew, which, unfortunately, didn't answer the main question he wanted an answer to—how to prove that Garfield Terwilliger killed his aunt.

He took a deep breath. "We've had a tension filled night," he said. "I suggest we go home and sleep on it. We can meet at the community center for breakfast and discuss it."

Ernie looked at his watch. "That won't be too long from now. It's already 2:15."

It seemed to Ed that they'd only been there for a few minutes. Whoever said that time only goes fast when you're having fun, had never crept around a dark garage in the middle of the night with only a thin metal wall between them and bad guys who might be capable of anything—including murder. He let out a deep breath.

"Let's make it brunch then," Ed said. "Meet you in the dining room at 10:00 am?"

Twenty-one

It was a quarter to three by the time Ed got home, undressed, showered, and got into bed. But, try as he might, he was unable to sleep.

He lay there—actually he tossed and turned—until 4:00, and finally gave up trying to sleep. He got up, shaved and brushed his teeth, and returned to the bedroom where he dressed by the dim light leaking through his curtains. Then he went to the living room and sat on the couch, leaning back and staring at the gray mass of his ceiling, letting him mind wander freely. Somehow, doing it sitting up was less disturbing than it had been lying in his bed.

The advantage of being awake was that he could order his thoughts, instead of being bombarded with snippets and scenes that appeared at random. As he did with any problem, he decided to start at the beginning and see if he could impose some order.

Beatrice Terwilliger's death would seem the logical starting point, but somehow his mind refused to anchor itself there. No, he thought, *that* was not what had started the cascade of events, it had been an outcome of the actual starting point—the changes she was making to her will.

How he knew this he was not sure, but he was convinced that the will was the key to the whole thing. He only had to find it, or determine its content. What had Zelda, or was it one of the Wertheim sisters, said? She'd taken the copy of the change from her *lawyer*, taken it home to read, and perhaps discuss with her heirs? He would need to get the name of that lawyer. There was, he knew, the matter of lawyer-client confidentiality, but that was a bridge he'd just have to cross when it presented itself.

Next was *how* she died. Again, he was operating on gut instinct, but his gut told him to trust Zelda and her belief that her aunt did not die from a heart attack. Well, he thought wryly, she did in fact die of a heart attack, but he was beginning to think that it had been induced.

Which led to *who*. Ed was convinced that Garfield Terwilliger was the guilty party. His problem was determining the man's motive and means, and whether or not he'd had the opportunity. Means would be almost impossible without a body, but if he could put him at the scene around the time frame of Beatrice's death, it would be useful. In fact, that was the crucial element—proving that he was in the house on the evening of May 26.

It was comforting to be able to organize his thoughts. It didn't matter that he didn't yet have the answers he sought, at least now, he had the questions in some kind of order. Most of all he appreciated order.

He glanced down at his watch, and realized that he'd been sitting there staring up at the ceiling for three hours. The time had zipped by unnoticed. In three hours he would be sitting down with Ernie and outlining his plan for getting answers.

Of course, that left him with three hours of time to fill. Ordinarily, he would have cooked breakfast, but that would mean he wouldn't feel like eating when he arrived at the dining room, and there was an unspoken rule at PVC, if you occupied a table in the dining room, you ate. He could go back to bed for three hours, but that would mean getting undressed and redressed, not a thought he relished. So, he spent two and a half of those three hours giving his house a thorough cleaning. By the time he was sure Ernie would be leaving his house to cross the street and walk with him to the community center the place was so clean he could have eaten off the floor.

He put his cleaning supplies away, exited the front door, and was locking it when Ernie stepped onto the porch. When Ed turned, Ernie's eyes went wide.

"Shit, man, you got bags under your eyes as big as steamer trunks. Did you get any sleep last night?"

Ed shook his head. "Nah, had too much on my mind. That's okay, though, I'll make up for it tonight. Probably sleep like the dead."

"I can believe that, 'cause you look like the walkin' dead right now. You know, we can bag breakfast if you want to go back to bed, you know."

"I don't sleep well during the day," Ed said. "I can make it till evening. Let's go get breakfast. Lack of sleep hasn't affected my appetite. I could eat an elephant."

Ernie shrugged and fell in beside him. They walked in companionable silence, taking their time. They arrived at the community center at five minutes before ten. The lobby of the community center was empty except for a single attendant at the desk, a tall, dark-skinned woman with what Ernie described as perky breasts and an attractive cornrow hair style. She smiled brightly at them as they passed. The dining room, when they entered, was sparsely populated, and their table near the window was unoccupied.

They walked to the buffet table where

Janet Murphy stood, holding a clipboard and making notes.

"Ed, Ernie," she said. "You two are late for breakfast this morning."

"We had a late night," Ernie said. "So, we decided to combine breakfast and lunch."

"We don't normally do brunch on weekdays, but the food line is open until 10:30, and luckily for you the crowd this morning was light, so there's a good selection left." She pointed at the warming trays of scrambled eggs, boiled eggs, bacon that was glistening with grease, biscuits, hashed brown potatoes, home fried potatoes, waffles, fried tomatoes, slices of cheese, ham and bologna, and at the end, two large containers of orange and tomato juice. They each took a large plate and loaded it with a bit of everything, and filled the largest available glasses with tomato juice, which they took to their table. They then went back and got coffee.

Back at the table, by tacit consent they spent the first three minutes eating without talking. Once the initial hunger pangs were satisfied, each sat back and lifted their coffee cups for long sips.

"Okay," Ernie said after he'd put his cup down. "What's your plan?"

Ed arranged two of the remaining three slices of bacon next to the small pile of hash browns and scrambled eggs.

"The way I see it we have two main

problems to solve," he said. "The most important one is to determine what's in that lost will."

"Yeah, but that's sorta like determining cause of death without a body, ain't it?"

Ed winced. He started to move the third slice of bacon into line with the first two, changed his mind, picked it up and held it in his left hand, biting from it as he made a row from scrambled eggs. "Almost forgot about that. We need to try and determine cause of death, 'cause if she did just die of a heart attack, the rest of the answers don't matter."

"I thought we already decided there was no way we could do that." Ernie rolled his eyes.

Ed finished the slice of bacon, and then used his fork to move some of the remaining hash browns to his mouth. He chewed slowly, twenty times, before swallowing. Then he put his fork down and leaned forward with his elbows bracketing his plate.

"I've been giving that some thought," he said. "Zelda said her brother's into drugs. Now, that means he's buying them from someone, and that someone probably has access to a lot of different kinds of drugs."

"What does that have to do with anything?"

"Remember Doc Vickers' boring lecture on the different things that can mimic a heart attack? Well, I'm no expert on street drugs, but he mentioned a couple I've heard of, cocaine and PCP, remember?" Ernie nodded. "If we can find Garfield's dealer, we can ask him what drugs he's provided."

Ernie reared back in his chair and laughed so tears poured from his eyes.

"What'd I say that was so funny?" Ed asked.

"You sure *don't* know diddly about how things work on the street, amigo. Even if you did know a drug dealer, you don't just go up to him and ask him what he's selling to someone else. That, my friend, is a good way to get your throat cut or a bullet to your brain."

"Oh, I hadn't thought about that. I guess I'll have to come up with some other way to figure out how she died. Of course, there's still the matter of her will. We need to find out what changes she made."

"Well, the only ones who would know that would be her, and she's dead, and her lawyer, and he probably couldn't tell you because of lawyer-client confidentiality."

"You're forgetting one thing," Ed said.

"Yeah, what?"

"If someone killed her, and I think that someone was Garfield, he took the changed will, so he'll know what's in it."

"And, you're just gonna get him to tell you?"

"It's not that simple . . . but, in a way, that's probably what we'll have to do. First, though, I would like to talk to her lawyer."

"Man, I already told you, he ain't gonna tell you nothing."

"I wouldn't bet on that," Ed said.

He did know that the lawyer wasn't likely to answer a direct question about the contents of Beatrice Terwilliger's changed will, or that he wouldn't give a direct answer. Lawyers were the ultimate, consummate bureaucrats, people for whom knowledge is power, and power is not freely nor willingly shared. He'd worked with many bureaucrats during his time at the Pentagon, some lawyers, most not. Some had been decent enough, but the ones he remembered most clearly were the ones who'd elevated bureaucratic gamesmanship to Olympic levels; the ones who worked their agendas— personal and otherwise—behind false smiles, evasive answers, and insincere flattery, kissing up, kicking down, and stabbing sidewise on their way up the promotion ladder. They had, though, a weak chink in their armor, most were susceptible to flattery. Even though they used it to get their way, they were taken in by it when they were the recipients. Ed knew that if he could get a meeting with Beatrice's lawyer, he could charm him into revealing something, probably just enough.

"I don't like that look on your face," Ernie said. "That look always spells trouble."

Ed smiled. *You have to break eggs to make omelets*, he thought, and almost said, but instead, he said, "We have another problem. We have to find out if Garfield was here Thursday night."

"Oh, you're just a fountain of interesting problems," Ernie said, sitting back in his chair. "There's no record at the entrance because he's on the list of frequent visitors who don't have to sign in, so how the heck are we supposed to do that?"

Before Ed could answer, a shadow fell across the table.

"Excuse us, gentlemen, but may we please join you?"

Charles Ray

Twenty-two

Patrick and Peter Ahearn stood there, silhouetted by the light fixture suspended from the ceiling, their hands clasped in front, looking, Ed thought, a bit like skinny versions of Tweedledee and Tweedledum from the 'Alice in Wonderland' movie. Ernie looked up at them and frowned. Ed's first instinct was to say no, that they were expecting Violet and Rose to join them, but they were halfway finished with their meal, so that would sound lame, and furthermore, the Ahearns had asked politely, which, as far as Ed knew, was a first.

"We'd understand if you don't want us to," Patrick said. "But, we'd like a chance to apologize for our . . . bad behavior."

Ernie's mouth dropped open.

"What bad behavior was that?" Ed asked.

Both Ahearns looked surprised. They shared a quick puzzled glance with each other.

"Well, uh, I mean . . . we took your table," Peter said. "We knew this was your favorite spot, and we should have asked if we could join you before."

"But," Patrick said. "We were afraid you might turn us down, so we came in early and took it. That was a rude thing to do, and we're sorry."

"So, if you think someone's gonna turn you down, you just go behind their back and take what you want?" Ernie asked.

"Well . . . yes, I guess that's what we did," Patrick said. "We shouldn't have done that. We were taught better, but everyone here can be so . . . aloof . . . we just figured you'd be the same. But, you came over and talked to us before. I know it was just to chastise us, but at least you spoke. So, we talked about it, and decided to apologize. I hope you'll accept it and allow us to join you."

Ed smiled. "Well, in that case, I reckon we'd be happy for you to join us."

"Uh, do you mind if we sit so we can look out the window?" Patrick asked.

Ed, who'd been sitting so he could see out the window and watch the entrance at the same time, scooted his chair around, leaving space so the two empty chairs could be arranged facing the window.

"Is that good enough?"

"That's perfect," Peter said. He and his brother sat down.

"Aren't you guys gonna eat?" Ernie asked.

They looked at each other and then at Ernie. "We ate breakfast before leaving home," Peter said. "But, I suppose we should have a cup of coffee so we're not violating Ms. Murphy's rules about not using the dining room as a lounge."

"I'll get us cups," Patrick said, rising. "Would the two of you like anything?"

Ed and Ernie shook their heads. He walked briskly to the buffet line where he poured two cups of coffee and returned to the table.

While the Ahearns sipped at their coffee, peering intently through the window, Ed and Ernie turned their attention back to their food. Ed, however, watched the brothers out of the corner of his eye, fascinated by their obsession with whatever lay beyond the window. Finally, his curiosity got the better of him. He put his fork down and turned to look out the window.

All he saw was a sea of green, red, orange, white and yellow, various shrubs, some flowering and some not.

"What are you guys looking for?" he asked.

"See those white flowers, the ones that look like spears?" Patrick said without looking at Ed. "The monarch butterflies that migrate through here like them especially for some reason. This time of day they're usually swarming all over them."

"Those are the big black and gold butterflies, right?"

"Actually, black and orange," Peter said. "Although there's the white monarch, which has gray where the orange should be, making it look sort of black from a distance. They account for about one percent of the monarch population."

"So, why're you guys so interested in this butterfly?" Ernie asked.

"Well, even though they're not an endangered species, widespread agriculture and use of pesticides eliminates many areas where they feed and breed, so they're of interest. Like bees and other insects, they're pollinators, but people don't appreciate it."

"They have a wide migratory range," Patrick chimed in. "From Canada to Mexico, so their potential impact on food production is huge. If all the butterflies and bees should become extinct, it'll have a catastrophic effect on worldwide food production."

"Shit," Ernie said. "Who'd have thought a little bug could be so important?"

"Exactly," Peter said. "That's why Patrick and I are participating in a project to monitor the monarch population and migration patterns. Of course, we've always been interested. In the evenings, for instance, we scout the area to see if we can spot gypsy moths. It's not as beautiful as the monarch or other butterflies, and its larvae are really destructive. Our monitoring of this creature is just the opposite of the monarch. We're checking to see if there is any increase in gypsy moth population, which could be devastating to agriculture, gardens and forests."

"So, you want to preserve one and eliminate the other?" Ed asked.

"Well, of course we want to preserve the monarch. As for the gypsy moth, we don't want to see it completely eliminated, just controlled to minimize the damage it does."

"Wow, I never realized what important work you guys were doing. You should have spoken up sooner, we would've been happy to have you join us here at this table."

Ernie didn't look as he totally agreed with that, but he nodded.

"So, you get around the community a lot, do you?" he asked.

"Yes, every evening," Peter said. "When the air is starting to cool, we often get an overlap with butterflies *and* moths at the same time."

Ed's eyes went wide. "You're out and about *every* evening? During what hours are you usually out?"

"We usually eat supper at 5:30, and are outside by 6:00 or 6:15," Patrick said. "We stay out until about 10:00 or 10:30. Moths are really nocturnal insects, they're attracted to the street lamps and the lights people have over their doors. We see more of them between 8:00 and 10:00 than any other time."

"I suppose you also notice people who are out and about, too, right?"

"Sure, but not too many people are out at that time of night."

"How about visitors, you know, people from the outside?"

"Oh, sure," Peter said. "But, there aren't that many evening visitors either."

"So, you'd remember them?"

Peter and Patrick looked at each other and smiled.

"Of course we would," said Peter.

"*All* of them? That could be a lot of people."

"Wouldn't matter how many," Patrick said. "We'd still remember them."

"When your job's cataloguing butterflies and moths, you have to have a good memory," Peter added. "You don't have time to look down at a notebook, because if you did, you might miscount. So, we make our observations, and then write them up later at home."

Ed felt a sense of anticipation. As much as he hated the phrase, it was like a light at the end of a tunnel.

"How about Thursday, May 26," he said. "Were you two out that evening?"

They both nodded. "Yes," Peter said. "The weather was a bit chilly, so there weren't many butterflies, but the moths were out in force, all over the place."

"Were you near the west end of Maple

Street at any time that evening?"

"Sure. Our house is on Jonquil, about midway between Cypress and Maple. We started around . . . oh, maybe 6:50 on Cypress, checking the vegetation along there down to Palm. We spent some time around behind the chapel. Lots of gypsy moths congregate in the trees there. Then, at around 7:45 we started at the east end of Maple and worked our way up to the garden behind here, then back down Maple to our street. We got back home around 10:45, I think, right Patrick?"

The other Ahearn nodded as he sipped his coffee.

"You know," Ed said. "That was the night Beatrice Terwilliger died."

"Yes, terrible that was. So sad."

"Even sadder is that she died alone."

"Well, at least she wasn't completely alone. I imagine she must have died after her visitor left."

Ed kept his expression calm, a difficult thing to do considering his excitement at where this conversation was going.

"She had a visitor?"

"Yes," Patrick said. "A young man. He arrived about the time we were passing her house on our way to the community center garden. When we passed it on our way home, though, his car was gone, so I guess it was just a brief visit."

"Did you get a good look at him?" Ed

asked.

"Not really. We were across the street, and only saw him from behind as he walked to her front door. He walked like a young man, average height and weight, and was wearing some kind of overalls."

Ed could feel his heart pounding.

"But, I remember his vehicle," Peter said. "What a horrible contraption. It was white or maybe gray . . . in that light it was hard to tell. Some kind of work van or something, because it had 'Garfield's Garage' painted on the side."

Ed shared a look and half-smile with Ernie. He felt like jumping up and hugging the Ahearn brothers. They might not have gotten a good enough look at Garfield Terwilliger to identify him, but their description of the van was enough to place him at the scene around the time of Beatrice's death.

One question answered, Ed thought, and it was the one he'd thought they hadn't had a snowball's chance in hell of answering.

Things were looking up.

Twenty-three

Ed and Ernie stayed in the dining room, talking and having coffee with the Ahearn brothers until Janet Murphy shooed them out at 11:55, complaining that the staff had to get the place ready for the lunch crowd which would start flowing at noon sharp. The Ahearns decided to go out to the back of the community center to see if there were any butterflies present. Ed and Ernie decided to drop in on Violet and Rose to discuss the case.

As they walked, Ed thought about the foolishness of not reaching out to people, and getting to know them. He'd avoided, nay shunned, the Ahearn brothers, thinking of them as oddballs and nuisances. After talking to them for a while, he found that they were actually quite nice, if a bit shy, and totally committed to conserving the environment. He could actually be friends with them. Even stranger, after an hour even Ernie had warmed to them and had invited them to the barbecue he was hosting in his backyard on the coming weekend. Violet and Rose would be surprised. Hell, they'd be shocked out of their support hose to see the Ahearns show up at Ernie's place.

They were passing between the high-rises when Ernie said, "You know, the Ahearns aren't so bad when you get to know them." As if he was reading Ed's thoughts. "I mean, except for their bug watching hobby, they seem like regular folks."

"Their butterfly and moth observations," Ed chided him. "Are important to the environment, they're doing a great service to the community."

"Oh yeah, I forgot, you're one of them tree huggers, too." At Ed's scowl, he raised his hands in mock surrender. "Okay, okay, sorry. I didn't mean nothin' by it. I'm all for saving the trees and stuff. Just sayin', though, that sittin' around watching bugs . . . er, butterflies, now that's a strange hobby for a man. I still like 'em anyway."

Ed chuckled. His friend was from the old school that believed that the earth was there for humans to exploit, and that nature was boundless, so why should people worry about cutting down a few trees or hunting a lion or two. It had taken Ed over a year of vociferous discussion—shouting arguments—to get him to finally concede that climate change was a reality. At least, Ed thought, he didn't vote Republican. He didn't think he had it in him to change that orientation.

"Different strokes for different folks," he said. "Hey, it's almost lunchtime, what say we drop in on Violet and Rose and cadge lunch from them."

"Now, that's a hobby I can get behind."

With a slight bounce in their step they kept going. When they passed between the high-rises, they veered right toward the south end of Jonquil Street.

As they drew nearer the Wertheim residence, Ernie began to walk slower.

"What's the matter?" Ed asked.

"Well, I was just thinkin'. Is it really such a good idea to drop in uninvited? I mean, what if they haven't prepared enough food for four people?"

"Then, they can just fix some more. Besides, all you have to do is bat your eyes at Rose, and she'll do anything you ask."

Ernie stopped so suddenly that Ed was two steps beyond him before he could stop. He turned to find his friend glaring at him.

"Just what is that supposed to mean?" Ernie asked.

"Aw, come on, you know . . . well, everyone else knows anyway . . . Rose is sweet on you. And, I've seen the way you look at her. You kinda like her too, don't you?"

Ernie's dusky cheeks darkened, not with

anger. "Naw, we're just friends," he said without an ounce of commitment in his voice.

"Maybe that's the way you see it, but right now, the way she sees it, we can drop in on her without invitation, and she'll be happy."

"What about Violet? That woman's heart's made of granite, or ice, I haven't quite decided which."

Ed smiled and slapped Ernie's shoulder. "Don't worry about her. She's a nosy puzzle fanatic like me. When I tell her what we learned from the Ahearn boys, she'll insist we stay for lunch."

"Good." Ernie breathed out slowly. "Let's open with that, so I don't have to do any eye-batting."

Laughing, Ed nodded. "Okay, I'll try not to put you on the spot."

The sun was at its highest point in the sky by the time they arrived at the edge of the neatly trimmed lawn surrounding the neatly maintained home occupied by the Wertheim sisters. Ernie let Ed precede him up the sidewalk, up the steps, and to the front door, and stood to the side as Ed pressed the brass doorbell button. The sound of the bell was a muffled musical melody from inside the house. The door opened with a slight 'woosh', and Rose Wertheim stood there, a white and yellow checked apron around her waist, and a white smudge on her left cheek. She smiled brightly.

"Well, look who we have here," she said,

looking mainly at Ernie who stood silently off to the side. "I told Violet we'd have guests for lunch."

"Uh, how'd you know?" Ernie asked.

"I just had a feeling." She stepped aside and motioned for them to enter. "We're having homemade chicken pot pie. I hope you like it." She still spoke to Ernie, even though Ed was standing closer.

Ed turned to his friend and smiled. Ernie's cheeks turned red.

"Oh," Ed said. "I'm sure he . . . we will. Can we help with anything?"

"You could open a bottle of white wine," Violet said from the entrance to the dining room. She, too, was wearing an apron, blue and white checked, but her angular face was unsmudged. "I know you prefer red, Ed, but white goes best with chicken, so that's what we're having." There was no arguing with her tone.

"I think they would both prefer beer, actually," Rose said, smiling at Ernie. "Right, Ernie?"

"Uh . . . yeah . . . no . . . I mean, white wine's fine with me. Don't go to any special trouble on my account."

"Sure, I'm fine with wine, too," Ed said. Truthfully, he didn't much care for white wine, but he was a guest in someone else's house, so it would be rude to be fussy.

Ernie and Rose seemed to be playing eye tag with each other, with Ernie blushing and

Rose's eyelashes fluttering like dandelion spores in a soft breeze. Ed had to clench his teeth to keep from laughing. They were like two kids in school who'd just run into each other, liked each other, but were too shy to say anything because their friends were watching, and they'd be teased if they let it be known. It was almost cute, but he wouldn't do or say anything to embarrass his best friend . . . no, strike that, friends. Ernie, Rose, and even Violet were the closest things to family he had, and despite Violet's acerbic attitude, which he knew was mainly put-on, he liked her. In fact, it was her blunt, no nonsense approach to life that he liked most about her. With Violet, what you saw was what you got, and if you didn't like it, tough on you. And, it was that 'get to the point' attitude that saved the day.

"We'll have the wine with the pot pie, and beer for after lunch," she said. "Now, come on in and shut the door. You're letting dust and insects in standing there gawking. And, get that wine uncorked. It's in the fridge."

Without waiting to see if her command would be obeyed, she turned and went back to the kitchen.

Ed and Ernie stepped inside the living room, and Rose shut the door.

"How'd you know we were coming?" Ed asked.

"Like I said, I just had a feeling. Violet won't admit it, but she was kind of hoping you'd drop by, too. We're hoping you can bring us up to date on what's happening with Zelda's situation."

Woman's intuition, ESP, or just the fact that they knew he was like a pit bull when it came to puzzles, it still amazed Ed that they would be thinking about the very reason he'd suggested to Ernie that they drop by. Maybe, he thought, that's what it means being friends with someone; you just know things without having to be told.

He smiled as he headed for the kitchen.

Charles Ray

Twenty-four

Lunch wasn't too bad, Ed thought, in fact, it was pretty darn good. The chicken pot pie was perfectly made, with small chunks of white chicken meat, slices of baby carrots, and sweet peas, in a thick white sauce, and he could smell a hint of ginger in it. The crust was thin, flaky, and golden brown. He managed to drink a glass of white wine, by dousing his pot pie with tabasco sauce and pretending the wine was grape juice that had turned a tad sour.

After helping Rose and Violet clear the table, the four of them retired to the living room, Rose and Violet with glasses of wine and Ed and Ernie with frosty bottles of *Dos Equis*, which the women stocked just for their visits. Petunia, the dead woman's Persian cat, who'd been prowling back and forth under the dining table silently begging for snacks, followed them into the living room, and ran immediately to a ball of yarn Rose had left in a corner, and began batting it about.

"Now," Violet said, as they arranged themselves around the coffee table, Rose and Violet on the sofa, and Ed and Ernie facing each other from the cushioned easy chairs on the long end of the table. "Tell us what you've found out about Zelda's aunt."

Ed noticed that she didn't refer to Beatrice by name. She'd probably, like him, never spoken to the woman more than once or twice, but he'd been trying all week to remind himself that she was more than just another resident of PVC. She'd been a living, breathing human being, and damned if it was right for her to be robbed of that humanity just because she'd died.

"Well, the death of *Beatrice Terwilliger* gets stranger by the day," he said. He noticed that Violet had flinched slightly at the way he'd emphasized Beatrice's name. Petunia stopped batting the yarn and stalked over to stand next to Ed's chair looking up at him. Damn, he thought, the cat recognizes her name, and is probably wondering where she is.

"Yes, well it's sad that we didn't get to know *Beatrice* better," Violet said, looking levelly at him. She caught his message. The ends of her mouth twitched up quickly and then settled back into their normal half frown position. "But, one can only hope that we can figure out how she really died."

"Those are my sentiments exactly, Violet."

He filled them in on what he and Ernie had learned about the various possible causes of death that could be mistaken for a heart attack, his suspicions about the cat locked in the closet and the arrangement of things at Beatrice's house, the missing will, and Ernie's suspicion that her nephew, Garfield was involved in illegal activities beyond buying and using drugs. Then, he hit them with the bombshell. "Ernie and I had breakfast with the Ahearns." Rose and Violet looked at him with brows raised. "They're really not bad when you get to know them." Ernie bobbed his head up and down. "Anyway, it turns out that they were out looking for butterflies and moths the night Beatrice died, and they happened to pass her house around 7:00 in the evening, and noticed that she had a visitor."

"A visitor; who would be visiting her at that time of the evening?" Rose asked. "Zelda was her most frequent visitor, and she was out of town that evening."

"Well," Ed said. "They didn't get a clear look at the young man . . . just enough to know that it was a young man, but they got a good look at his vehicle. From their description, it matches the one Garfield Terwilliger has at his garage."

"But, that's not proof," Violet said. Sure, leave it to her to be the one to throw up an objection. "Unless it's a really exotic car, which I doubt that young man can afford, it probably matches any number of similar cars in this area."

It was slightly annoying, but Ed appreciated it, because it was a good way to make sure they'd considered all angles and didn't jump to unwarranted conclusions. Of course, this time, the conclusion was warranted.

"Yeah, but how many of them have 'Garfield's Garage' painted on the side?"

"Oh," Violet said. "I see what you mean. So, Garfield was there the night she died. Was he there during the time she died, before, after?"

"We can't be absolutely sure. Dr. Vickers made an educated guess about time of death. I imagine he could be off by a good bit at both ends, but I'm willing to guess that he was."

"You know what that means," Rose said.

"I only met that boy once, but I always knew he was a bit off," Violet said.

Ed held his hands up like a traffic cop at a busy intersection.

"Hold it, folks. Let's not rush to judgment. We can only put his vehicle there, not him, at least not definitely. Besides, we need a motive before we can start accusing him of murder."

That brought silence to the room. It was the first time any of them had used the 'M' word, but there it was, and this, they knew, was some serious stuff. Even though the state of Maryland had repealed the death penalty in 2013, getting convicted and sent to prison for killing your elderly relative wouldn't make you a favorite of other prisoners, Ed reasoned, although, doing it for money might ameliorate some of their ire, especially the career criminals among them. Still, he thought, you don't just accuse someone of murder lightly. There was a little thing called evidence, motive, and the like.

"So," Rose said. "What could his motive be?"

"I imagine what the motive is for most murders," Ed responded. "Financial gain, of course; he did it to get her money."

"So, he killed the old lady for his share of her money?" Ernie asked.

"That'd be my guess." Ed tapped his index finger against his chin. "Of course, without knowing what's in her will, it's just guessing. Nothing we can take to the authorities."

"Damnation, that skunk could get away with murder," Ernie said, sputtering. "That ain't right."

"Suppose we could find out what was in Beatrice's will?" Rose asked.

Everyone's head swiveled in her direction, three pairs of eyes bored into her. Unaccustomed to being the center of attention, she shrank back against the sofa cushion. Petunia, who had been trying to nuzzle against Ed's trouser leg unsuccessfully, because he'd been pushing her back—gently, of course—looked up at Rose, cocked her furry, white head to one side, then walked daintily over and jumped up into her lap and nuzzled her head against Rose's breasts, which had the effect of drawing everyone's attention away from her and toward the cat.

"I swear," Violet said. "That cat's the most sensitive creature I've ever seen. It's like she can read your thoughts and feelings, and she understands *everything* you say."

Rose, the cat cradled in her left arm, idly stroked its back with her right hand. Petunia arched her back and purred loudly.

"She certainly does seem very perceptive," Ed said. "But, Rose, back to you. What'd you mean about finding out what was in the will?"

"Well, I was thinking that we could just contact Beatrice's lawyer. According to Zelda, he drafted the original as well as the change, so he should know what's in it."

"Of course he would," Ed said. "But, I imagine that attorney-client confidentiality would mean he wouldn't be able to share it with us."

"Oh, I hadn't thought about that." Bright spots of red blossomed on her cheeks.

"What if Zelda asked him?" Violet asked.

Ed thought that one over. Though something of a barrack's lawyer, his actual knowledge of the law was a mile wide and an inch deep. Unfortunately, the information about attorney-client privilege was below that inch.

"I really don't know," he said. "But, you know, it wouldn't hurt to ask. Do you think we could get her to do it right away?"

Charles Ray

Twenty-five

It turned out that they *could* get Zelda to do it right away or as close to right away as could be expected from one in her line of work. One of the advantages of being a drummer in a band that played at obscure clubs up and down the coast from Wilmington, Delaware to Raleigh, North Carolina is that most of the work was at night, usually very late at night, meaning that Zelda and her fellow musicians didn't usually hit the rack until four or five in the morning, and slept until one or two in the afternoon.

She had just rolled out of bed, and was about to step into the shower when Rose called and made the proposal. She agreed immediately, gave them the Rockville address of her aunt's attorney of record, John Montrose, and promised to meet them there at 3:00 pm. Violet and Rose insisted on going along, which Ed would ordinarily have objected to, but it made it easier to argue for using his 4-Runner instead of Ernie's pickup, so he agreed to that, hoping the lawyer wouldn't be put off by having such a large entourage invade his office.

The four of them, with Violet and Rose occupying the back seats, set out at 2:30, giving adequate time to get into Rockville's city center, find parking, and meet Zelda at the lawyer's office.

John Montrose, Attorney-at-law, had an office in a two-story white, wood frame house on North Washington Street near West Middle Lane, north of West Montgomery Street. Built in the 1920s, the house had a wrap-around gallery on the first and second floors, both of which had been tastefully screened in and converted to extra office space on the second floor, and waiting rooms on the second. The original front door had been widened, so that the reception area was actually on what had been the structure's front porch. It was within walking distance of the courthouse complex on Maryland Avenue, located on the site that once housed the Rockville Regional Library. They found parking in a commercial garage just up the street, as the six parking slots in the cracked concrete parking lot adjacent to Montrose's office were all taken. Ed offered to drop everyone off, but they insisted on staying together, so the group, a bit bedraggled from the afternoon warmth, walked through the front door into the reception area at 2:59. Zelda was standing at the receptionist's desk waiting for them.

In keeping with the age of the building, the reception area was traditionally furnished. The receptionist, a middle aged woman with her gray-streaked blonde hair pulled back into a neat bun, and dressed in a light blue pant suit, sat behind a plain mahogany desk. She pushed her gold-framed glasses up on her nose as they approached, and opened her mouth to speak.

"That's okay," Zelda said. "They're with me. Hi, guys, did you find a place to park nearby? I had to park in the grocery store lot up the street and walk myself."

Not to be outdone in her own milieu, the receptionist smiled wanly and said, "Very well, then. Mr. Montrose will be with you momentarily, so if you'd just have a seat." She waved a perfectly manicured hand toward a group of lightly cushioned chairs across from her desk. On the wall behind one chair—what had once been the outer wall of the building, but was now the back wall of the reception area—was a large black and white framed photograph of F. Scott Fitzgerald, author of *The Great Gatsby*, who, though originally from Minnesota, and a long-time resident of New York and Hollywood, was buried in the cemetery of the Catholic church adjacent to the Rockville Metro Station, along with his wife, Zelda—Ed could not help but chuckle at that coincidence, earning puzzled looks from the others, who apparently hadn't made the connection—who died in a fire at the mental institution somewhere in the south—he could never remember whether it was North Carolina or Georgia, everything south of Richmond being the Deep South to him, and therefore, terra incognito—where she had been committed for years.

When Zelda sat in the chair underneath the picture, Ed chuckled again.

"What's funny?" Ernie asked as they took seats facing her.

"Yeah, Ed," Zelda asked. "What tickled your funny bone?"

He pointed up at the picture. Zelda twisted around and craned her neck to look up at it.

"Do you know who that is?" Ed asked.

"No, maybe one of the dudes who founded this law firm," she said, shaking her head.

"No, you're wrong. That's F. Scott Fitzgerald."

"Who?" She looked at him as if he'd just spoken in Mandarin.

"F. Scott Fitzgerald, the writer," he said. "He wrote *The Great Gatsby.*"

"Oh yeah, I saw that movie. Leonardo DiCaprio was pretty good in it, but I liked him better in *Titanic.*"

Ed rolled his eyes. American kids these days, he thought. They no longer have to read anything worthwhile in school, what with teachers having to teach mainly to standardized tests, so their knowledge of the world came from TV, the movies, video games, and what they read on the Internet. Teachers could no longer give homework, had to worry about assigning reading, for fear they would be accused of exposing students to non-politically correct literature—heaven forbid they be asked to read anything by Mark Twain—and, regardless of how poorly students did, they were passed from grade to grade, and out into the world, many of them barely able to complete a driver's license application without help. How, he wondered, have we continued to prosper as a nation? Oh yeah, we have some pretty smart immigrants coming from places like India and China to do the technical and scientific stuff, and some hard workers from other places, like Latin America to do the manual work that most Americans refused to do.

"Anyway," he said. "That's who the picture is of. Fitzgerald was considered one of the greatest writers of the 'Jazz Age.' In fact, he's the one who coined that term."

She looked at him with an open-eyed, arched-eyebrow look that told him she had no idea what he was talking about. He decided to change the subject.

"Do you think the lawyer will tell us what was in your aunt's new will?" he asked.

"Gosh, I sure hope so, or this trip will

have been like a total waste of time."

'Do you think,' Ed wanted to say, but he realized that he couldn't really blame Zelda. She was a product of her time. Not given to introspection or deep thought. She seemed a good-hearted person, if a bit shallow. The cat liked her, though, and Ed trusted animal instincts. If an animal accepted you, you couldn't be all bad.

"Yeah, me too," he said.

He was saved from further conversation by the arrival of John Montrose, or as the sign to the right of the entrance proclaimed, John Montrose, Esq. He often wondered why lawyers in the twenty-first century persisted in using a title that was passé in the nineteenth, but like politicians insisting on being 'the honorable' this or that, he guessed it was their way of setting themselves apart from the hoi polloi. *That's what we've come to, a society of US versus THEM, and when the THEM isn't clear, we make up designations, or add titles to achieve that extra bit of exclusivity.* He realized that he was doing just that himself, ruminating on an inconsequential matter like the title a person put with his name, and shook himself mentally to bring his attention back to the matters—well, matter really—at hand.

John Montrose, dressed in a brown suit that hung loosely on his frame, the coat unbuttoned and draped over the paunch that hid his belt buckle, and with dark brown scuffed wingtips, looked like Ed's idea of a small-town lawyer from a fifties movie than someone who would be practicing law in the shadow of the nation's capital. It was interesting, Ed thought, that, unlike most slightly overweight people whose clothing strained to contain their bulk, Montrose's clothing was at least a half-size too large, making him look like he was losing weight. *A neat little trick. This guy's smarter than I would've been prepared to give him credit for.*

He had a round head, with thinning brown hair, flecked with gray and combed over but not really concealing his severely receding hairline, watery blue eyes that seemed to bore right through you, and thin, unsmiling lips pursed as if he'd just sucked on a lemon. He made a beeline for Zelda, extending a pudgy, liver-spotted hand.

"Ms. Terwilliger," he said in a resonant voice that didn't fit his appearance. "Sorry if I kept you waiting." He glanced around at the other four. "Is someone talking care of you folks?"

Zelda stood and grasped his hand. "No, Mr. Montrose. They're with me. And, please, I've had my name officially changed; I'm now just Zelda."

Montrose frowned and his face got the pinched-up look of someone who has just smelled a particularly noxious fart, but is trying not to let everyone know it.

"Uh, yes, now I remember your aunt

telling me that you were doing that. Sorry . . . Zelda . . . and, please accept my sincerest condolences for your loss. Beatrice was one of my oldest clients." His cheeks reddened. "Uh, I mean, one of the clients I worked with the longest."

"That's okay," Zelda said, smiling. "She was pretty old, too."

"Ah, but like wine, she only got better with age." The man had a wistful look on his face. Ed wondered if the relationship had been more than just lawyer and client. He cleared his throat.

Montrose shifted his attention from Zelda to the rest. He frowned, creating three waving furrows in his high brow. "As to . . . I'm not sure it's appropriate for outside parties to be present at our discussions."

"Oh, these guys are like family." Zelda turned and beamed at Rose and Violet. "They've been really helpful, and anything you tell me, they can hear."

He didn't look convinced.

"Violet and Rose were Aunt Bea's closest friends," she said.

Ed knew that wasn't the whole truth or at least, he thought so, but if it got them an audience with the lawyer, he wasn't going to tell anyone that Zelda was fibbing. "And, Ed and Ernie here, well they're helping me with a problem I have about Aunt Bea's death."

Twenty-six

Mentioning 'problem' to a lawyer is like saying 'heel' to a well-trained dog; it gets their attention. Ed had learned that much working occasionally with the Pentagon lawyers. They hated it whenever someone started a meeting with a 'problem.'

Montrose cleared his throat. "Well, perhaps we should go to my office and talk in private." He turned and headed inside the building proper, and the five of them followed behind him like ducklings following mama duck.

The interior of the building had been extensively remodeled. Downstairs, which when it was originally built had contained living room, dining room, kitchen and sun room, had been converted into a law library and offices for the firm's paralegals. Off to the right, just inside the original entrance, was a staircase to the second floor which had contained three bedrooms and two bathrooms, which were now being used by Montrose and his two associates, Melvin Cohen and Bryan Marquette, two younger lawyers. As the older man, and principal of the firm, Montrose's office was the former master bedroom in the back right corner with two large windows overlooking the fenced-in backyard. He had his own full bath, while his younger associates and their clients used the bath that between their two offices on the left side of the building.

He led them past the closed doors to the double doors of his office, and ushered them inside.

The bathroom door was to the right. To the left, the doors had been removed from the large walk-in closet, and a wet bar installed on one side and a wall table, underneath which was an efficiency apartment-sized refrigerator, on the other. Opposite the door was a large mahogany desk with a high-back leather chair behind it. A floor to ceiling bookcase filled with thick volumes was on the right and a meeting area consisting of a small rectangular table and six chairs was on the left. The floor was covered in a cushiony carpet in green and gold abstract patterns. On the walls, were pictures of Montrose with some people Ed recognized and some he didn't. Prominently displayed on the wall behind the desk, right of the window, were two framed certificates, his diploma from the

University of Maryland, and his law degree from Harvard. Below the Harvard diploma was a certificate attesting to his having made the Harvard Law Review, whatever that was, but whatever it was it indicated that Montrose was probably a bit more than the country lawyer he appeared to be from his attire. To the left of the window two photos hung; one, a smaller version of the one in the reception area, and the other of an attractive lady with a page boy style haircut and dressed in what Ed remembered was called the 'flapper' style from the early part of the century. He assumed that, since the man in the photo was F. Scott Fitzgerald, the woman was his wife, Zelda.

Even though there were no ashtrays in evidence, Ed detected the smell of burnt tobacco, not the stale odor of cigarettes, but the musty-sweet odor of pipe tobacco. Montrose didn't flaunt his habit in front of clients, perhaps, but he also ignored the government rules against smoking inside places of business.

Montrose motioned for the five of them to take seats at the table, and asked if anyone wanted coffee or tea, which everyone declined. As they were taking their seats, Zelda introduced everyone again, pointing to each as she said their names.

When everyone was seated, with Montrose at the end of the table nearest his desk, he leaned forward with his chin resting on his steepled fingertips.

"Again, Ms. . . . Zelda," he said. "Please accept my condolences. Your aunt was more than just a client. I thought of her as a friend. She'll be missed."

"Yes. Except for my brother, she was the only family I have." Zelda flicked at a tear in the corner of her eye.

Montrose cleared his throat, his brow furrowed as if he was deep in thought. Ed's gaze wandered from those around the table to the two photographs.

"Ah, Mr. . . . Lazenby, you seem to be interested in my photographs. I noticed you looking at the one outside in the lobby as well," Montrose said.

"Yes, Fitzgerald is one of my favorite authors."

Montrose smiled. "Well, I'm impressed. You're the first person to recognize him."

"Yeah," Zelda said. "Ed's an expert on this Scott Fitzgerald dude."

"Actually, it's *F.* Scott Fitzgerald," Montrose said. "Well, his full name was Francis Scott Key Fitzgerald."

"Named for his cousin, Francis Scott Key," Ed said. Montrose's smile broadened and his head bobbed up and down.

"Who is that?" Zelda asked.

Ed's eyes rolled back in their sockets.

"Key Bridge? The Star Spangled Banner? Do either of those ring a bell?" he asked.

"Yeah, I know where Key Bridge is, and I

know what the Star Spangled Banner is. Man, that's one hard song to sing."

"Well, what they have in common is that one is named for, and one was written *by* the same person, Francis Scott Key," Ed said. "And that Francis Scott Key was a cousin of the author F. Scott Fitzgerald."

"That is truly impressive, Mr. Lazenby. I assume you've read most of his works? Which was your favorite? *The Great Gatsby*?"

"Well, I admit *The Great Gatsby* was good, but the one published after his death, *The Love of the Last Tycoon* was, in my opinion, his greatest work. You seem to be a great fan yourself."

"I am, but I'm also family; on his wife Zelda's side. The Alabama Sayre's . . . that was Zelda's maiden name . . . originally came from New York. My mother was a granddaughter of one of the Sayres who stayed in New York. So, in addition to liking his work; and hers too for that matter; you could also say these are family photos, as I'm unmarried and have no other family to display."

"Now, that's what I call impressive," Ed said.

Montrose put a hand over his mouth, but his cheeks had turned ruddy. "Why, thank you. I think, though, we should get to business. What can I do for you, Zelda? You mentioned having some kind of . . . problem?"

She took a deep breath and locked intently at the lawyer. Ed was impressed that she had the presence of mind to do that. Her outward appearance, the hair, the makeup, the clothing; even the weird way of talking; were not at all indicative of the mind in that skull of hers.

"Mr. Montrose, I understand that my aunt was changing her will?"

"Why, yes she was. Didn't she discuss it with you?"

"I . . . I was supposed to talk to her the day she . . . died." She wiped a drop of moisture from the outside corner of her eye. "My band had an engagement that night, so I made arrangements to see her on Friday . . . but, but—"

He inclined his head toward her. "I'm so sorry. So, you never saw the changes?"

"No, and even worse, I can't find a copy of it at her house."

"Are you sure? It's really only two pages long, it could easily be misplaced."

Zelda's brows curled and nearly bunched together over her nose. "You know my aunt, Mr. Montrose. You know how unlikely that it."

"Yes, now that you mention it that is hardly likely." He chuckled and made eye contact with Ed. "Beatrice was a *very* organized person, one could almost say obsessively so. She had a specific place for everything, and insisted that everything be in its proper place. It would be so unlike her to misplace an important document. My goodness, who am I kidding; it would be unlike Beatrice to misplace *anything*."

Zelda placed her hands on the table, palms down.

"Ed and I searched her house thoroughly," she said. "Not only could we not find the changed will, we couldn't find her copy of the original will, and I know she had one because I've seen it before."

Montrose steepled his hands again, a worried look on his face.

"That greatly complicates matters," he said. "It wouldn't matter about the original will being missing, because I have a copy, which is the one I would use for probate anyway. But, I'm aware of her intent to *change* her will, and as her attorney and an officer of the court, I'm bound to respect her wishes. Unfortunately, she had me make only one copy, which she took with her after I drafted it, and without that copy, it will be difficult to overturn the original will should it be contested."

Ed raised his hand like a student asking to be recognized in class.

"Yes, Mr. Lazenby?" Montrose said, smiling wanly at him.

"Is there any reason to think the original will might be contested?"

Ed watched Montrose's brow furrow as the man looked at him through half-closed eyes.

He could sense the wheels turning in the man's mind. Probably, he thought, trying to figure what the mountain of rules for lawyerly conduct, written by other lawyers, allowed him to say, and what it prohibited him from saying. Finally, Montrose's expression relaxed, his lips turned up in a half-smile. His gaze shifted to Zelda. "You're familiar with the provisions of your aunt's original will, correct?"

"Yeah, she like left everything to me and my brother, Garfield, split down the middle."

"Essentially, yes," he said. "But, her new will changed all that."

"She changed the percentage of our shares?"

"No," was all Montrose said as he looked levelly at her.

Suddenly, Ed thought he knew what the lawyer was doing. He wasn't *telling* her anything. He was answering her questions. Now, if only she would ask the *right* questions.

"Is one of us getting everything?"

Good girl, Ed thought.

"No, not really."

Zelda's eyes narrowed to slits and her brow wrinkled. Damn, Ed thought, she's hit a wall. He wondered if it would be appropriate to help her frame the questions, and then decided, why the hell not. "Ask him if you're both out of the will," he said. He saw the half-smile again, which Montrose quickly stopped.

"Well, were we?" she asked.

"I'm not at liberty to disclose the specifics of her will until we're in the probate hearing," Montrose said.

As good as a 'yes,' Ed thought. Luckily, he was sitting next to Zelda, so he was able to lean close and whisper in her ear, "Ask him where your aunt's money *was* going."

"Who *was* getting everything?" she asked.

"Her estate was to go to something she loved very much."

That pulled Ed up short. He didn't know enough about Beatrice Terwilliger to even guess—or, did he. His mind flashed back to the search of the place he'd made with Zelda, and the pictures all over the place. He *did* know one thing that she liked. The woman liked cats. But it couldn't be that easy. Would she leave everything to some organization related to cats, or would she, as Montrose said, leave it *to something she loved very much.* He leaned in and put his lips next to Zelda's ear. "Ask him if she was leaving everything to her cat," he whispered.

Zelda gave him a wide-eyed, quizzical look, saw he was serious, and turned to the lawyer. "Did she leave everything to Petunia?"

Montrose's eyebrow gave a little wiggle. He looked intently at Ben, then back at Zelda. "I can neither confirm nor deny that," he said.

Bingo, Ed thought. She was leaving her estate to her cat. That, of course, meant that someone would have to be designated trustee for it, since a cat can't open a bank account or work an ATM. He decided to cut out the middle man and be direct.

"Who did she designate as trustee for the estate?" he asked.

Montrose gave him that half-smile again. "Again, I'm neither confirming nor denying, but for the sake of argument, if she did indeed decide to leave her estate to her pet cat . . . Petunia . . . she would have to select a trustee. I *can* tell you that she did not identify that person to me . . . that is, assuming that is what she was deciding to do, of course."

Zelda was now looking totally confused. Ed would have to explain it to her later, though. He was now smiling at Montrose who was struggling to keep a neutral expression on his face.

"I would assume . . . just for the sake of argument," Ed said. "That she would probably pick someone she knew well, and someone who was familiar with the animal."

"For the sake of argument . . . that would be the logical thing to do."

It all began to fall into place for Ed. He had the motive and he was pretty sure he had the opportunity elements of the crime nailed down, now all he had to do was determine means and he could tie everything up in a nice bow and present it to Carl Janzen.

"Mr. Montrose," he said. "On behalf of

Zelda, I want to thank you for your time. You've been a great help." He stood. Everyone but Montrose looked at him with questions in their eyes. "Mr. Montrose is a busy man, and we've taken up enough of his time. I think we should go now."

Still looking puzzled, they stood. Montrose stood and walked to the door of his office, and opened it for them.

"I'm sorry I couldn't be more helpful," he said. "But, you must understand that legally, my hands are tied."

"Yeah, sure," Zelda said. "When will the will be probated?"

"I'll let you know." As they exited, he motioned with a nod of his head for Ed to hang back. When Ed came abreast, he leaned in close, "You're a very perceptive man, Mr. Lazenby. I do hope you'll be discrete in how you handle the *information* you gleaned from today's meeting," he whispered.

"Not to worry," Ed whispered back. "I don't think anyone else figured it out. They're used to me coming up with hair-brained ideas, so when I tell them they'll never figure it came from you."

Montrose laid a hand on Ed's arm. "Do let me know how this all works out."

"As soon as I've figured it out myself," Ed said.

Charles Ray

Twenty-seven

Since they were already downtown, and it was getting late, Ed convinced everyone to join him for supper at a Thai restaurant on Rockville Pike near the Twinbrook Metro Station. After a great meal of *som tham, pad thai, and tom yam gung,* washed down with sweet and tangy Thai lemonade, Zelda went home and Ed and his crew drove back to PVC.

Ernie invited him to drop in for a nightcap, but Ed begged off, saying he had some serious thinking to do, and didn't want to crowd his brain with alcohol. After promising that he would join the three of them for breakfast in the community center at 7:30 the next morning, he dropped Rose and Violet off, and drove home, dropped Ernie off at the end of the driveway, and then pulled into his garage.

He thought he'd be too keyed up to sleep, and did spend the first ten minutes in bed going over in his mind what Montrose had 'told' him, but going into minute number eleven, sleep sneaked up and closed over him like a tsunami.

At 6:00, his usual time, he woke up. The transition from asleep to awake was as quick as if someone had flipped a switch, and if he'd dreamed, he didn't remember it. He'd gotten less than eight hours sleep, only six to be exact, because it had been nearly midnight when he got into bed, and he'd spent that ten minutes thinking over what he'd learned from John Montrose, but he still felt refreshed when his eyes snapped open. None of the blurred vision, cotton ball in the mouth feeling, and for once, when he rolled out of bed his joints didn't creak and pop. Any morning that he woke up without the pains that unfortunately came with getting older was a good morning in his book.

By 6:50 he'd done three of the four S's that had been a daily routine when he was in the army; shit, shower, and shave; deciding to wear his brown suede loafers so no 'shine' was required, just a little brushing to make them look neat. They went well with the brown Dockers and his green cotton North Face shirt, casual with just a hint of rugged elegance. He spent a few seconds admiring himself in front of the full-length mirror on the inside of his closet door, happy to see that, even though he was beginning to go gray at the temples, and had a bit of spread around the middle, he still looked pretty good—hell, for a man his age, he thought, he looked *damn* good.

When he stepped out onto his front porch, Ernie, dressed in faded jeans, a white polo shirt with a blue and yellow collar, and a pair of white and blue Nike Air Max low tops, was already coming up the driveway.

"You're looking spiffy this morning," Ernie said.

"So are you. The ladies are gonna love us in the dining room."

"Well, let's not keep 'em waiting."

Laughing, they crossed the street to the graveled trail that led between the high-rise condos to the community center.

As they emerged from between the two high-rises and were about to cross Ash Street, Ed noticed Violet and Rose turning the corner onto Ash Street. Rose was waving to get their attention.

"Hold up, Ernie, here come Rose and Violet. Rose is waving to get our attention." He laughed. "If I hadn't turned my head, though, I wouldn't have noticed."

"You know how Rose is," Ernie said. "She doesn't like to raise her voice."

Ed snorted. "Yeah, unlike Violet, who doesn't mind raising her voice, even indoors. Sometimes I wonder if they're really sisters."

Then again, he thought, siblings can be as different from each other as strangers; witness Zelda and Garfield Terwilliger. Both of them came from the same gene pool, and, he assumed, were raised in the same household, but were as different from each other as sweet corn was from asparagus.

Rose was puffing and Violet was frowning when the two women came alongside them.

"Why didn't you come by and walk with us?" Violet asked. To Ed, it sounded more like a demand than a question, though.

"Uh, well, I figured you two would be along soon," he said. "I didn't want to disturb you too early."

"What? You think we weren't going to make the 7:30 appointment? We were going to be late . . . what, because we're women?"

"Yeah," Ernie said. "You're al—"

"Not at all," Ed said, interrupting him before he'd completely inserted his foot into his mouth. "I'm sorry. We should have come by, but if you must know, I just didn't want to do all that extra walking."

Ernie gave him a funny look, which he tried to ignore. Violet 'huffed' a couple more times. "Hah! You two go to the golf course and walk, what, two or three miles, but you can't walk a few extra yards to our house?"

"Uh, well, when you put it that way, I guess we do sound pretty bad."

"Hmph, you want to hear how bad I really think you are –"

"Nah," Ernie said. "I put my big foot in my big mouth, and I humbly apologize. Can we just go get some breakfast and hear what Ed has planned next?"

"Yes, I agree with Ernie," Rose said. "Arguing before you eat is not good for your digestion."

"Rose, you just made that up," Violet said.

"No, I think she's right," Ed said. "I read it somewhere. But, Ernie's right, too. I have an idea how we can solve this whole case . . . if anyone cares to listen."

"Of course I want to," Violet said, looking down her nose at him. "Why else do you think we're here so early?"

Ed held out his arm. "Well, in that case, shall we proceed?"

Still frowning, Violet took his arm and they started across the street. Ernie started to follow, but saw that Rose wasn't moving, but was looking from him to her sister and Ed, her brows raised.

"Oh, yeah," he said, walking back to her and offering his arm. "Shall we join them?"

She smiled demurely and linked arms with him.

The lobby was empty except for a middle aged man at the reception desk. He had a bored look on his florid face, and paid them no attention as they passed, instead picking idly at the prominent veins on his bulbous pink nose. The dining room was sparsely populated, no more than three tables with occupants. The heady aroma of fresh baked bread and pastries, the woody smell of bacon and sausage that filled the room had not yet been tainted with the smell of menthol and old age that the room had when it was fool.

Janet Murphy was standing near the entrance.

"Good morning," she said, beaming them a broad smile. "Ed, Ernie, you'll be happy to know we have buttermilk pancakes this morning, and they're still fresh and hot. Violet, Rose, it's so nice that the two of you could join us for early breakfast. I think you'll find everything fresh and hot just the way you like it."

Violet growled an unintelligible response. "Good morning, Janet dear," Rose said. "I'm quite sure everything will be lovely."

Murphy looked at Violet with a worried expression. It hadn't been that long ago that Violet had been quite critical of the food provided by the community's chief dietician; of course, that had been before Roland Vickers had finally caved and hired a professional chef for the kitchen. The worry furrows on Murphy's brow, though, made it clear that she hadn't forgotten. She wasn't the greatest cook, but Ed thought her food was okay. While in the army he'd eaten a lot worse. But, he had to admit that since the new chef came on board, the food had gotten a lot better.

"I've not seen a thing to complain about

lately," Violet said. Her voice was stern, but Ed saw a twinkle in her eyes. Dang, Ed thought, she's just yanking the poor woman's chain. He pinched the inside of Violet's arm just above the elbow. "Ow, that hurt." But, she got his message. "Actually, Janet, the food's really, as Rose said, quite lovely."

With a relieved smile, Murphy ducked her head and spun around to return to overseeing the two women stocking the buffet line.

"Violet, you should really stop being so cruel to Janet," Ed said as they made their way to the table near the window. "She works so hard. And, the food is really good."

"I know that. I'm just having a little fun with her. Don't worry, I'll get her something really good for Christmas, and maybe even for her birthday. Rose, remind me to check with the HR people to find out when her birthday is."

Ed pulled a chair out for Violet, while Ernie did likewise for Rose, seating the two women between them so they all had a view of the buffet line. Ed sat so he could also see the entrance.

"Okay," Ed said. "How are we gonna do this? I know; Violet, you and Rose get your food and coffee first, and then Ernie and I will get ours."

"I thought you said you'd made peace with the Ahearns and they wouldn't be snatching your table anymore," Violet said.

"Yeah, but someone else might try it. Better safe than sorry.

Just as Violet and Rose stood, Janet Murphy arrived at the table carrying a tray upon which was a coffee pot, creamer, sugar container and four large cups. "I brought you some coffee," she said as she put it in the center of the table. "That way you won't have to carry so much when you get your food."

Ed knew that this wasn't something she did for just anyone. She was probably doing it to kiss up to Violet, or maybe she was just so stunned that Violet had been . . . nice to her, this was her way of saying thanks.

"Why, Janet dear girl," Violet said. "Aren't you just the sweetest little thing?" Rose leaned over and kissed her cheek. Murphy's cheeks flamed red, and her eyes almost crossed.

"W-why, t-thank you, Violet . . . . I hope you, all of you, enjoy your breakfast."

"Think nothing of it, dear. It's us who should be thanking you for your fantastic service."

Violet turned to Ed and winked. A totally flustered Murphy walked back to the buffet line, tottering slightly like someone who has had a bit too much to drink; not quite drunk, but a tad unsteady. Ed chuckled, thinking that Violet was absolutely incorrigible.

"She's never gonna change," Ernie said when he was sure she was out of earshot. "She's just playing with poor Janet now.

There's no way she meant all those compliments."

"Maybe, but I'm not so sure sometimes. I think Violet's all bark and no bite."

Violet and Rose were back quickly. Rose had a modest amount of food on her plate, while Violet had a four-stack of pancakes, hash browns, and bacon *and* sausage. The aroma coming from her plate caused Ed's mouth to water.

"Okay, guys," Violet said. "It's your turn."

"I hope you left something for us," Ernie said, looking at her plate, and getting a snort in reply.

Ed and Ernie returned to the table, their plates making even Violet's look empty. She looked at them, an expression of smug satisfaction on her face.

"I see you found a new supply of food," she said. "What'd you do, go to the kitchen and bribe the cook?"

Everyone ignored her Ed and Ernie began digging into the stacks of pancakes and piles of bacon and potatoes as soon as they sat down. There was no conversation for a few minutes as Ed, Ernie, and Violet devoured their food, while Rose daintily picked at hers, only the sounds of metal utensils striking porcelain dishes, and the occasional sound of lips smacking—not Rose, never Rose, who would never be so gross, and who winced each time her sister or one of the men did.

The bite of their early morning appetites

blunted, and nearly half of the food on their plates gone, the three of them slowed to Rose's pace, and then stopped eating entirely. They put their forks and knives down and began sipping occasionally the coffee Murphy had brought.

Violet took a long sip, wiped her lips with the back of her hand, causing Rose to wince again, put her cup down and leaned forward with her bony elbows resting on the table to either side of her plate.

"Okay, Ed Lazenby," she said. "What are you doing to help Zelda solve her problem? I can see the way those sneaky eyes of yours are twinkling, you have something on your mind."

Ed took his time sipping his coffee. He put his cup down and wiped his lips with his napkin, and then put the napkin back across his lap.

"As a matter of fact, I do have some ideas," he said. "I have an idea what happened to Beatrice . . . I don't have all the details yet, of course . . . and I'm working on an idea to smoke out the culprit." He moved his plate slightly to the side, making a clear space on the tablecloth. "In order for it to make sense, though, I need to bring everyone up to speed on this rather complicated situation."

Violet scowled. "Are we going to have to listen to one of your long, boring history lessons before we get to the good stuff?"

Ernie just looked at him blankly. The two

of them often rehashed things they were working on, looking at them in a historical perspective. In many ways, Ernie's mind worked like Ed's, it needed to lay things out occasionally and look at them in order to make sense of the world. Rose just looked on with her usual expression of amused whimsy.

"I promise you," Ed said. "It won't be *that* long, and I assure you it will *not* be boring. What it will do is help us catch the culprit."

"That's the second time you've said culprit," Violet said, her scowl changing to a look of interest now. "Does that mean you think a crime was committed?"

"Oh yes, there was a crime all right, it was murder . . . murder most foul."

"Oh my goodness," said Rose.

"Who is the culprit?" Violet asked.

Ed held a hand up. "Let's not get ahead of ourselves. I believe that once I've explained what I've learned, and what I surmise, the name of the culprit will be apparent." He reached for the salt and pepper shakers, then shook his head and picked up the syrup and catchup containers instead, which he placed next to each other in the space he'd cleared. He then put the mustard container behind them. "Here, we have three people. I won't name them just yet. First, let me tell you a little story."

He picked up the mustard container and placed it to the side.

"Here we have . . . Mustard . . . Mustard

has a lot of money, and must decide what to do with that money." He tapped the syrup and catchup. "Syrup and Catchup here are Mustard's only relatives." He then picked up the toothpick holder and placed it next to the mustard container. "Well, except for Toothpick, who, while not actually related, is Mustard's closest companion." He looked around the table, and was pleased to see that he had their undivided attention.

He put some space between the catchup and the syrup.

"Now, ordinarily, Mustard would leave everything to Catchup and Syrup, shared equally, but for some reason decided not to. Instead, Mustard decides to leave everything to Toothpick."

Ernie let out a little 'yip!' and slapped the table. "I get it, now. Mustard is Beatrice Terwilliger, and Catchup and Syrup are Zelda and Garfield, but who the heck is Toothpick?"

"Why, Toothpick must be Petunia," Rose said in that quiet voice of hers. "Beatrice was leaving all of her money to her cat. That's what that lawyer meant yesterday when he said she wanted to live her money to something she loved, right?"

Ed didn't want to expose Montrose, so he just nodded, and said. "That's kind of what I figured out. I mean, she really loved that cat, right, and he did say she was leaving her money to *something* she really loved, not *someone.*"

"Then, that means that both Zelda and Garfield were being cut out of the will," Violet said. "That would certainly be a motive to get rid of Beatrice and destroy that new will. But, that also means that Zelda has as much motive as her brother. Could the two of them be working together?"

"Violet, how can you say such a thing," Rose said in a pained voice. "You can't believe that Zelda would do such a terrible thing. She loved her aunt."

"Yes, but money can make people do terrible things."

"True," Ed said. "But, I agree with Rose. I don't think Zelda would harm her aunt."

"But, this Garfield's another kettle of fish," Ernie said. "I wouldn't trust him as far as I could throw him."

"I don't really think Zelda's guilty of anything, but I don't know her brother," Violet said. "And, of course, we have nothing to tie him to Beatrice's death."

Ed opened his mouth to speak, but was interrupted by the arrival of Peter and Patrick Ahearn, smiling down at him.

"Hello, folks," Peter Ahearn said. "Do you mind if we join you. The weather today's perfect for swarming, and we'd like to observe the bushes outside the window here."

Violet frowned and began to speak, but Ed raised a hand to stop her. "Of course, guys," he said. "We'd be happy to have you join us.

In fact, I have a proposal to make to you, to all of you."

Just like that, an idea had popped into his mind. Ed knew how he was going to solve the mystery of Beatrice Terwilliger's death.

Twenty-eight

Ed got up early Saturday morning. He showered, shaved, and dressed quickly and made a light breakfast of toast, scrambled eggs and coffee, and after eating it got on the phone to make arrangements for what he expected to be a busy Saturday and an exciting weekend.

The first person he called was the lawyer, John Montrose, and after explaining why he called and what he planned to do, invited him to come to the late Beatrice Terwilliger's house at PVC just before noon. Next, he called Violet Wertheim, and asked her to invite Zelda to come at 11:30 and invite her brother to come at noon. The reason for the invitation, he explained to her, was that the lawyer wanted to discuss the will with them, and felt it best to do it outside his office, hoping that would make them curious enough not to ask questions. His final call was to his friend, Ernie, with special instructions involving the Ahearns.

He spent the next two hours cleaning and dusting his house, even though it didn't really need it. The activity helped him to keep his enthusiasm in check. He wanted to be absolutely calm when he confronted Garfield.

At 11:20, his phone rang. It was Violet calling from her hand phone. "Ed, Zelda and her brother just arrived," she said in a hushed voice. "What should I do now?"

Damn, not only were they early, but he'd hoped they would arrive separately so that he could talk privately with Zelda. Oh well, he thought, he'd just have to improvise.

"Just keep them occupied. Montrose should be arriving in a bit. I'll come over soon."

"Okay, but hurry. This Garfield character makes me nervous."

"Careful, Violet, he might hear you and become suspicious."

"Don't worry. I'm in the kitchen making tea. Zelda's keeping him occupied in the living room."

She broke the connection quickly. Ed then called Rose and gave her some special instructions. Satisfied that his plan was so far working, he looked around, took a deep breath and walked out his front door, to the sidewalk, and turned left toward Maple Street.

As he approached Terwilliger's house, he spotted Ernie and the Ahearns standing behind some shrubbery at the corner of Jonquil and Maple. Ernie flashed him a thumbs up sign which he acknowledged with a wave. He walked up to the front door and rang the bell. Zelda answered the door.

"Ed, glad you could make it," she said. "Mr. Montrose isn't here yet, but Violet's made some tea. Would you like to join us?"

"Don't mind if I do," Ed said, stepping inside.

Garfield Terwilliger was sitting on the sofa. He'd changed his gray overalls for a pair of jeans and a maroon Washington Redskin's tee shirt. A cup of brown liquid sat on the coffee table in front of him. He sat stiffly, with his knees together and his right foot, clad in a scuffed pair of running shoes, tapped silently on the carpet. When he looked up and saw Ed, he blinked and scowled.

"What the fuck's he doing here?" he said.

Violet sat on a chair facing him, holding a cup of tea in her hand. She was dressed in a sleeveless yellow blouse and baggy brown pants. "Watch your language, young man," she said.

Garfield blinked and his cheeks went red. "Uh, sorry, ma'am." He looked back up at Zelda. "Did you invite him, Zelda? This is a family matter. He's got no business bein' here."

Zelda balled her hands into fists and planted them on her hips. "I can invite whomever I please. He's a friend of mine, just like Violet, and I want some friendly faces here with me when the lawyer arrives."

"If you ask me, this whole thing's just a waste of time. Why couldn't Montrose just invite us to his office during business hours?"

"I'm sure he has his reasons," she said. She walked to the coffee table and picked up the teapot and an empty cup. "Would you like a cup of tea, Ed?"

"I believe I would." Ed took the chair opposite Violet, sitting where he could see Garfield from head to toe. "I see you're not drinking your tea, Garfield. Don't you like tea?"

The young man looked down at the cup in front of him and flinched. "Nah, I'm a coffee drinker." He ran his palms over his thighs as he spoke. Despite the fact that the air conditioner was going full blast—in fact, the room felt cool to Ed—his brow glistened with sweat. Zelda, on the other hand, just looked like . . . Zelda. She looked curious, but not a bit nervous. It wasn't quite enough to convince Ed his theory was right, but it added to his sense of confidence that he was on the right track.

"I can make you a cup of instant coffee,"

Violet said. "There's some in the pantry."

"That's okay, I'm good." His right foot began tapping again.

"You seem a bit nervous," Ed said. "Is everything okay?"

His gaze bored into Ed, but the muscle under his right eye was twitching. "Yeah, everything's fine. I just have things to do. I can't waste my morning sitting 'round here."

The doorbell rang. Garfield bucked, rising almost an inch off the cushion, his eyes darting toward the door.

"That's probably Mr. Montrose," Zelda said, rising and heading toward the door.

"It's about damn time."

"I told you to watch your language, young man." Violet's tone brooked no argument. Garfield tucked his chin into his chest and pouted at her.

Zelda was back quickly with John Montrose in tow. The lawyer smiled at Ed and Violet, and nodded at Garfield who only looked sullenly back at him. Zelda went into the dining room and came back with a straight back dining chair which she placed across from her brother at the coffee table. Montrose straightened his jacket, put his briefcase on the floor under the table and sat. He looked at Ed expectantly.

"Well, Mr. Lazenby . . . Ed," he said. "You want to tell us why you invited us here?"

Garfield lunged forward, glaring first at Ed, then at Montrose. "I thought you were the one who called this meeting."

"No," said Ed. "Actually, I am the one who set this up."

Garfield's hands shook as he stared daggers at Ed. "What the fuck's this about, old man?"

"I'm not telling you to watch your language again, young man."

"Fuck you, old lady."

Fists clenched, Violet started to rise. Ed waved her to sit. She huffed, but sat. Ed turned his attention back to the young man.

"Consider yourself lucky that I interceded, young man," he said. "You really don't want to be messing with Violet. Now, if you can control your tongue, I'll explain why I arranged this little tete a tete."

"It's your show, dude." Garfield sat back and folded his arms across his chest, tucking his hands in under his arm pits, and staring down at his knees.

Ed sat back in his chair. All eyes, except Garfield's, were on him.

"Okay, let's start with the matter of your aunt's will. Correct me if I'm wrong, Mr. Montrose, but despite the fact that the copy of Beatrice Terwilliger's changed will is missing, she informed you that she wanted the changes, and that in effect negates the original will?"

"That is essentially correct," Montrose said. "She made known to me, her attorney of record, her desire to change her will. I drafted the new will and gave the only copy to her to bring home and discuss with her legal heirs. And, then it was her intention, as stated to me, to sign it. I would, of course, notarize and file it." His gaze swept over Garfield and Zelda. "Since she never told me she didn't want to make the changes, in effect the new will reflects her wish, and I'm legally bound to respect that."

"Meaning what?" Ed asked.

"Meaning that the original will is effectively null and void. It will be complicated because we no longer have the paper copy of the new will, but I do have my notes, and will use them in the probate hearing."

"Y-you mean she's disinheriting us?" Garfield's eyes were wide and his fists were beating a tattoo on his thighs. "That ain't right!"

"How do you know the new will disinherited you?" Ed asked calmly.

Garfield's mouth opened and closed several times like a beached fish gulping for air. He looked at a point to the right of Ed's head. "Uh, I'm j-just assuming that if she changed her will, she took me and Zelda out. Why else would she change it?"

"Are you sure it's not because you *saw* the changed will when you visited your aunt on May 26?"

"Hey, I already told you, I haven't been here in weeks. I didn't see her then, and I sure as hell didn't see no will."

Ed stood. He smoothed out the crease in his trousers. "Well, why don't we just see if you're telling the truth, shall we?"

He turned and strode to the front door.

Twenty-nine

Ed stopped at the door and looked over his shoulder. Garfield Terwilliger sat hunched on the sofa with a confused look on his face. Shrugging, Ed opened the door.

Across the street, Ernie stood on the sidewalk flanked by Peter and Patrick Ahearn. Ed waved for them to come over, and turned, holding the door open for them.

When the three men entered, only Violet showed no reaction to their presence. Zelda and Montrose looked, brows raised in query, Garfield looked up, scowled, and looked away. When the Ahearns were inside the door, Ed stepped between them and placed a hand on each shoulder.

"Ladies and gentlemen," he said. "Allow me to introduce Peter and Patrick Ahearn.

They're residents of Potomac Valley Community, who also happen to be quite experienced naturalists. Their area of expertise happens to be butterflies and moths, which they monitor frequently throughout the community.

Now, Zelda and Montrose were looking thoroughly confused. Violet had a half smile on her face.

"They are, I must point out, quite experienced observers; they have to be to be able to distinguish different species of butterflies and other flying creatures. Their observations of the moth population cause them to be out and about, often quite late in the evening. During one of their expeditions, or perhaps explorations is a better word, on the evening of May 26 to be precise, they made an interesting observation. Would anyone care to guess what that was? No. Well, why don't I have them tell you? Gentlemen, would you please tell our guests what you saw on Thursday, May 26?"

The Ahearns exchanged glances. Peter nodded.

"Well, we were looking for swarms of Gypsy moths that night," Patrick said. "We started out down near the chapel."

"I think he wants to know what we saw up in this area, Patrick," Peter said.

"Oh, yes, of course. Well, it must have been sometime between 7:45 and 8:00; we were checking out the hedges across the street near the corner, when we saw someone get out of a light-colored van and enter the front door of this house."

"You have a light-colored van, don't you, Garfield?" Ed asked.

"Yeah, along with a thousand other people in this area," he answered without looking up.

"What can you tell us about the van other than its color?" Ed asked.

"It had 'Garfield's Garage' painted on the side," Peter said.

"Not many of those, I'll wager," Ed said.

Sweat was rolling down Garfield's cheeks now, and both of his feet were tapping the carpet. He did not return Ed's stare.

"There's one other thing," Patrick said. "We were across the street with Ernie when the young man there arrived, and even though he's not wearing those coverall things, I recognized him from his body structure and gait. This is the man I saw entering this house on May 26."

"Most definitely is the same person," Peter chimed in.

Garfield's face was now pale, and his arms were wrapped tightly around his chest.

"You old farts can't be sure of what you saw," he said, but his voice lacked conviction. "That time of day, the light's not all that good and old folks like you don't have good eyes anyway."

Montrose was now looking at Garfield

through narrowed eyes.

"I disagree, young fellow," Ed said. "In fact, the Ahearns have excellent eyesight, and are experienced observers, but you might be able to convince some people they could be mistaken and that you're not lying about being here that night."

"He's correct," Peter Ahearn said. "Both Patrick and I have 20/20 vision. Our eyes were checked just a month ago, in fact."

"So, there you have it. Now, you might be right that someone would argue that even with 20/20 vision, they couldn't be absolutely certain it was you they saw on May 26," Ed said. "That's why I have one more little test for you . . . Rose, you can come in now."

Rose Wertheim came in from the kitchen through the dining room where she'd been waiting for Ed's summons. She clutched the hatbox tightly to her chest. Ed motioned for her to stop just inside the door.

"Zelda, would you please go over to Rose?" he asked.

Looking puzzled, Zelda rose from the sofa and walked over to stand next to Rose, who lifted the lid to the hatbox. Zelda smiled and reached inside the box. As she started to withdraw her hand, Rose leaned close and whispered something. Zelda looked confused, but withdrew her empty hand and went back to her place on the sofa.

"Now, Garfield, would you do what Zelda

just did?"

"What for?" Garfield's face was screwed up like a petulant child refusing to eat his vegetables. "What kinda game you playin'?"

"Humor an old man, please. It's just a little experiment. It won't hurt you."

"Come on, Garfield, I just did it, and nothing happened to me," Zelda said.

Garfield sank back into the sofa cushions. "This is stupid. Why the hell are we wasting time like this, and what the fu-, er, frick does it have to do with Aunt Bea's will."

Ed noticed that he'd not said his aunt's death, just the will. In fact, he hadn't seen the first sign of grief from the young man during any of his encounters with him.

"Trust me," Ed said. "This little experiment has everything to do with what we're here for. Please, just humor me this one time. I promise you it won't hurt."

Still looking petulant, Garfield heaved himself up from the sofa and with his shoulders stooped, approached Rose. Under his breath, Ed said, "At least, I hope it doesn't hurt."

When Garfield was within three feet of her, and reaching for the hatbox, it began to quiver in her arms. She was looking at Ed. He nodded. She flipped the lid open.

No one was prepared for what happened next, least of all Garfield Terwilliger. A ball of white fur burst from the hatbox, and attached itself to his chest. A screeching 'meo-o-o-owr', followed by an ear-piercing scream filled the room.

Garfield stumbled backwards, hit the corner of the chair Violet was sitting in and landed with a thud on his butt, grabbing at Petunia who had attached herself to his chest and was scratching and yowling and generally creating pandemonium.

"Get her off me! Get this fucking cat off me," Garfield screamed.

Zelda leapt from the sofa and jumped across the coffee table. She reached down and grabbed Petunia, lifting the Persian and cradling her against her chest.

"There, there, Petunia," she said. "Everything's gonna be okay."

The cat snuggled its head against her cheek and began purring. Zelda looked down at her brother who was still on his back with a look of panic on his face. The front of his tee shirt was in tatters, with parallel lines running diagonally from near the shoulder to just below the sternum. Some of them were red-streaked where the cat's claws had found flesh, but there were also slightly older scars, still a bit red and puffy, and beginning to show black scabbing at the edges..

Ed walked over and looked down at the quivering man.

"Looks like the cat doesn't care for you very much," he said. "She got you good, she did. I'd get that looked at right away if I was you, and I'll bet dollars to donuts that you got those other scratches about a week ago, right?"

Zelda, still stroking Petunia, looked from Ed to her brother.

"Garfield, what's he talking about?"

He glared back at her, a murderous look in his eyes. "I shoulda killed that mangy fucking cat when I had the chance, insteada just locking it in the closet. Never understood what Aunt Bea saw in the damned thing."

Charles Ray

Thirty

Zelda's face went pale. Her lips trembled. Her eyes glistened. She clutched Petunia tighter against her breasts.

"Garfield, no," she said. "Tell me you didn't . . . not Aunt Bea; how could you?"

He pushed himself into a sitting position, and glared up at her.

"She was cutting me out of the will," he said. "I would've gotten nothing."

Tears began flowing down her cheeks. "We were both being cut out, but, but, that's no excuse to—"

"Actually, Zelda, that's not entirely true," Montrose said.

Everyone, everyone that is but Ed, looked at the lawyer who had swiveled his chair around to face Zelda and Garfield.

"I don't understand . . . wasn't she leaving everything to Petunia." She continued to absently stroke the purring cat.

Montrose nodded. "Yes, she was, but she was going to name someone to be the custodian of the cat and the estate. That was what she wanted to be sure of before she signed the changed will; that it would be someone who would love Petunia as much as she did, and would take care of her for the rest of her life. Of course, when the cat dies, whatever's left in the estate then goes to the custodian. From the looks of it, I think it's safe to say you would have been her choice to administer the estate."

Zelda looked dazed. Garfield banged his fists against the floor. "No, that can't be," he said, dots of spittle flying from his mouth. "You don't have that change. I'll contest it. If Zelda's getting anything, I deserve something too."

Montrose stood and adjusted his jacket, looking down at Garfield as if he was a pet accident on the carpet. "I'm afraid, young man, that you have no standing to contest the will," he said. "You see, even if Beatrice hadn't changed her will, you would get nothing."

"Wha-, why? I'm a blood relative the same as Zelda, and I'm the oldest."

"Doesn't matter. You've just confessed to killing your aunt in front of seven witnesses, eight if you count Petunia. You can't profit from a criminal act. So, you see, even if Beatrice hadn't changed the will, Zelda would get everything."

All the air went out of Garfield. He flopped onto his back and covered his eyes with his arms, and began crying.

"Damn, damn, damn," he said between sobs.

"I guess it's true," Ernie said. "Crime really doesn't pay."

Ed walked over and knelt next to the supine man.

"Why'd you do it, son? Why on earth would you want to kill your aunt?"

Garfield looked almost vacantly at him. There was a trace of anger in his eyes, but mostly there was just the hollow look of defeat.

"I didn't mean to do it. I was comin' to ask her to loan me some cash to help me out of a little bind I'm in, but she called and asked me to come over. I thought that was a good sign . . . but, that old woman had other things on her mind.

He wiped at his nose. It was dripping snot like a faucet with a slow leak, a little rivulet snaking down over his quivering upper lip.

"Before I could even ask her for money, she was showin' me that fuckin' will. Said she was cutting me out 'cause of the way I treated that fuckin' fur ball."

He glared at the cat clinging to Zelda.

"What did you do to Petunia?" Ed asked gently.

"When I got here, that cat kept tryin' to crawl up on me," he said. "I asked Aunt Bea to put it in another room, but she said she wanted to see how I got along with it. I mean; what the fuck'd that have to do with anything, right? So, I grabbed the stinking thing and when it started scratching me, I locked it in the front closet. Fucker scratched my chest somethin' awful, it was so pissed off. Aunt Bea was pissed off too. That's when she went and got that damn will and showed it to me. Said only somebody who got along with *Petunia* could be in her will. Then she wrote Zelda's name on it and signed it. Said Petunia was getting all her money, and Zelda would be responsible for takin' care of things. I mean, can you believe that shit? I'm a blood relative too, and I been runnin' errands for that old bag for years."

"But, Garfield," Zelda said. "Aunt Bea was there for us when our folks died."

"So what . . . ain't that what family's supposed to do? We were just kids. She couldn't just leave us out on the street."

Everyone else watched, shocked looks on their faces, as he almost calmly described the events of that fateful evening. Ed, however, felt that something in his narrative was missing. He walked back to his chair and pulled it around in front of Garfield. He sat with his hands on his knees and leaned forward; a stern look on his brown face.

"You said your intention when you came was to borrow money from your aunt," he said. "Did you intend to kill her after she gave you the money?"

Garfield cringed and shook his head. "Naw. That was an accident. I didn't know she'd react to that shit the way she did."

"React to what?"

"I put some PCP in her tea when she went to her bedroom to get the will. It was just supposed to knock her out and give me time to toss the place, you know, get whatever cash she had layin' around, maybe some jewelry. She drinks that nasty smellin' mint tea with lotsa honey, so I figured she'd never notice the PCP. I thought it'd just put her to sleep for a while, and when she woke up, she wouldn't remember shit, you know. It didn't work out that way, though. She musta only drunk half a cup before that shit hit her. Man, it was freaky. Her eyes went wide, and she grabbed her chest. I mean, I barely caught that fucking cup before she dropped it. Then, she just keeled over dead. Wasn't nothin' I could do for her, so I just grabbed that will, and then I went to her bedroom and got the other copy and got the hell out of here."

"Where did you get this . . . PCP?"

"I, uh, got it from Jerry Stark . . . well, actually, I got it from Turk, but Turk works for Jerry."

"Is this Stark person your usual drug supplier?"

Garfield gave Zelda a dark look. "I guess you told him, huh, little sis?" Zelda   sniffed and buried her face in Petunia's fur. "Yeah," he said. "Jerry's my supplier. He's also the dude I chop cars for. Problem is, I owe him more for drugs than I pull in at the garage, even with the chop shop operation, and he been pressin' me for his money. I told him I could get it from my aunt, 'cause she's loaded. So, he gave me the PCP. Only it didn't work out, and now he's gonna break my knees if he don't kill me."

Ed almost felt sorry for him. "Not necessarily," he said. "Look, Garfield, you're going to jail for what you did to your aunt, but this Stark person is also responsible, and he's into other illegal activity as well. I think the police would be interested in what you can tell them about him."

Garfield looked up at Ed, something like hope in his glistening eyes. He smiled. Ed felt like smashing his fist into that smile. He stood before he could give in to the temptation.

"Well," Montrose said. "This has been a most interesting morning. Zelda, I think probate of your aunt's estate will proceed smoothly once the legal dust settles." He turned and smiled at Ed. "Ed, thanks for including me in this. You know, you're quite the detective. You mind if I call on you should I need something looked into?"

"Uh, I'm not a licensed private detective," Ed said.

"Oh, it wouldn't be anything requiring a

licensed investigator. Just cases that are, shall we say, in need of someone who can think and act outside the box. I'd pay you the usual fees for your time, with expenses."

"I'll think about it and get back to you."

He'd already thought about it, but he'd always been taught never to appear too eager. He'd call Montrose sometime later the following week.

"I think someone should probably call the police," Rose said.

Charles Ray

Thirty-one

The sky was gunmetal blue with a scattering of wispy white clouds. A cool breeze blew in from the north, rustling the leaves of the stately trees lining the streets of Potomac Valley Community.

Ed and Ernie had gotten together for breakfast, and then Ernie had gone back to his house to change, while Ed went into his bedroom and stuffed himself into a dark blue suit—one he hadn't worn in years—polished his black wingtips until they shone like glass, brushed his hair until the tight curls flattened out a bit and turned to waves. Looking, he thought, like a slightly disreputable backwoods preacher, he left the house, just as Ernie, in a dark gray suit and looking just as uncomfortable as he felt, crossed the street. He looked at his watch. It was 9:20, forty minutes before the memorial service for Beatrice Terwilliger was to begin.

"Should we walk down and accompany Rose and Violet to the chapel?" Ernie asked.

Ed shook his head. "No, you know Violet likes to be fashionably late, and Rose goes along with whatever big sis decides. They'll show up a minute or two after ten, watch and see if they don't."

Ernie shrugged and started trudging toward Cypress Street. Ed fell in beside him. Together they walked in silence in as much in the shade of the towering oaks and maples as possible toward the chapel at the east end of the village. A few people at their end of the community were also getting an early start. They nodded and exchanged greetings as they passed them. Ed, from his years in the army, and Ernie, who'd walked a postal route for decades, tended to be purposeful walkers, far too fast for most of the elderly residents of PVC, so no one joined them.

Ed hated attending funerals, and even though this wasn't technically a funeral with body, casket, and all the foofaraw that goes with such ceremonies, he knew that some old lady would start sniffling—probably someone who'd never spoken a word to Beatrice when she was alive—and he'd feel like shit for the rest of the day. He'd been just a smidgen excited by the events of the previous day. He'd called Carl Janzen and reported what

Garfield Terwilliger had told them. Within an hour the burly detective, accompanied by two squad cars of uniformed Montgomery County cops, was outside the Terwilliger house. The blinking red and blue lights of the squad cars, and the obvious 'policeness' of Janzen's official vehicle drew almost as many gawkers out of the houses along Jonquil, Maple, and Wisteria Streets as the ambulance that carted Beatrice's remains away had. Heads bobbed and fingers pointed when Garfield, handcuffed and sagging between two cops, was hauled to one of the squad cars and taken away, followed closely by the second car.

Janzen had stayed for thirty minutes after they left, having quickly recorded the repeat of Garfield's rambling confession, and took statements from each of them.

"We'll get your statements typed up and call you to come in and sign them," he said when he'd finished. He looked squinty-eyed at Ed. "On second thought, they'll probably be done by Monday afternoon. I'll bring them here for your signatures." He swiveled his head to take in Zelda and Montrose. "I'll have an officer come to your residences to get your signatures." They both nodded. He looked back at Ed and Ernie and slowly shook his head. He opened his mouth as if to speak, and then shook his head again, stuffed his recorder and notebook into his jacket pocket. After stabbing the two of them again with a piercing gaze, he spun on his heels and left.

"I have a feeling he's gonna wanta have a long talk with us on Monday," Ernie said.

"You think?" was all Ed could say.

Ed didn't feel like talking now. He wanted to be anywhere but the chapel, be doing anything other than sitting in an uncomfortable pew listening to someone eulogize a woman he'd never met, or if Vickers conducted the service, that he hardly knew. He only hoped the man wouldn't ask the attendees to say anything. Never fond of public speaking, he was petrified at the idea of having to stand up in church—a place he seldom went—to say anything.

Only a few people were ahead of them when they reached the church, but they slowed down to allow them to enter first. In deference to the age, and in some cases the infirmities, of the residents, there were only three steps up from the walk to the front door of the chapel, and for those in wheelchairs or using walkers or canes, there was a four-foot-wide ramp to the side. The double doors of the entrance were open wide. When the way was clear, they mounted the steps and stepped inside.

A cold blast of air from the building's central air conditioning hit them as soon as they passed under the lintel. Wasteful, Ed thought, running the A/C on full with the doors open, but he supposed many of those already seated in the high-backed wooden pews needed the fresh, cool air.

The chapel was nondenominational, holding services at different times and on different days for those who refused to attend the generic nondenominational services. The symbols of the various religions were probably kept in storage, brought out when needed, but now, except for the stained glass windows, with cherubs and roses; the two rows of wooden pews with a carpeted aisle down the middle; and the dark wood pulpit, raised slightly above the main floor and backed by a small choir area with more uncomfortable looking wooden benches and an organ off to the right were the only things that marked this building as a place of worship. The area beneath the pulpit was bedecked with flower arrangements, mostly white lilies, no doubt provided by the various clubs and activity groups in the community.

About fifty people were already inside and seated, mostly toward the front. The front row of pews on the right was empty, probably, he thought, reserved for family, of which there was only one left. At first Ed didn't see Zelda, but as he and Ernie were about to slide into the back row of pews on the right, he saw a pale arm waving from the front. Even when she stood up, Ed didn't recognize her at first. The streaks were gone from her hair, and now it was light brown and cut short, just edging over her ears; her makeup was lightly applied, and she was wearing a black dress that highlighted her youthful figure. When he smiled in recognition, she beckoned him to come to the front of the chapel.

"You and Ernie please sit with me," she said in a quiet voice. "I called Violet and Rose, and they said they'd join us when they arrive, and Mr. Montrose will be coming along soon."

"I don't know," Ed said. "I imagine the front row's reserved for family."

Her eyes teared up, and she sniffled. "With Garfield in jail, you guys are the only family I have left." She looked as if she would burst out crying.

"Well, in that case, we'd be honored."

He was rewarded with a smile and she reached out and grasped his hand, pulling him down beside her on the bench. Ernie moved to sit on her other side. From behind him, Ed could hear hushed whispers. Even though he couldn't make out the words, he was pretty sure his exploits in solving the mystery of Beatrice Terwilliger's death was the subject of the discussions.

Zelda hooked her arm around Ed's and leaned against his shoulder. "Thanks for coming. I don't think I could have taken being here all alone much longer." He patted her hand. "What are they planning to do . . . I've never been to a memorial service before."

"Neither have I," he whispered into her ear. "I imagine someone will get up and tell us what a nice person your aunt was and how we'll all miss her."

She smiled and looked up into his eyes. "Someone who probably never met her, right?"

"It's the thought that counts," he said, patting her hand again.

Ed's attention was attracted to a rustling sound behind him. He looked back to see Violet and Rose rushing down the aisle toward them. He looked at his watch. It read 9:59. He looked over at Ernie who was also looking toward the two sisters and held up his watch.

"You pegged them, amigo," Ernie said.

The sisters walked past them, each giving Zelda a brief hug before seating themselves to Ernie's right. Rose, Ed noticed, was carrying the hatbox in her left arm, hugging it against her hip as she hugged Zelda with her right. She settled it on the pew between her and Violet.

"What's in the hatbox?" he whispered at her, even though he had a sneaking suspicion he already knew.

She lifted the lid slightly. A pair of round, curious eyes surrounded by white fur peered through the space between the lid and rim. Ed's eyebrows rose.

"Petunia's part of the family, too," Rose whispered. "It's only right that he be here. Don't worry, he'll behave."

Ed only shrugged. Why not, he thought,

it's not as if that's the strangest thing to ever happen here.

"Where's that lawyer of yours, Zelda?" Violet asked, not bothering to whisper.

"Mr. Montrose said he'd be here."

As if on cue, the lawyer, dressed in an expensive looking black suit, looking more like a big city lawyer, Ed thought wryly, appeared at the end of the pew. He looked a bit flustered.

"Sorry I'm late," he said. "Traffic from Rockville was terrible. I've never seen it this bad on Sunday before."

"Don't worry," Ed said. "The service hasn't started yet." He looked at his watch; 10:05. "In fact, it's late."

Montrose shook Ed's hand, hugged, and then, shook hands with the others as he made his way down the pew to sit next to Rose. His eyes widened at the sight of the hatbox, but he said nothing.

As soon as Montrose was seated, there was a rustling and murmuring from behind them. They looked back to see Roland Vickers, dressed in a shiny black suit, pearl shirt, bright red tie, and shiny black shoes, making his way up the aisle, nodding to people as he passed them. Ed sniffed. The man was turning the memorial service into a spectacle about him, which wasn't surprising. Roland Vickers was, Ed knew, a blatant self-promoter who took every opportunity to draw attention to himself and his position. The man was absolutely shameless.

When Vickers got to the front pew, he moved in front of Zelda and dropped to one knee in front of her and took her hands in his, causing the rustling and murmuring to increase in volume.

"Ms. Terwilliger," he said. "I just want you to know that we here at Potomac Valley Community share your loss. Your aunt was a valued resident who will be greatly missed." He looked at Ed. "And, I want to personally apologize for any trauma my incorrect diagnosis of the cause of your aunt's death might have caused you. I really have no excuse for what was sloppy medical work, but I do hope you can forgive me."

Zelda pulled her right hand free and placed it on his shoulder. "There's nothing to forgive, Dr. Vickers," she said, patting his shoulder. "You called it like you saw it. Mr. Montrose tells me that almost any doctor would have come to the same conclusion you did under the circumstances."

"Still, I should have been more careful." He looked at Ed. "Trust me, in the future I will. If not for the ingenuity of our own Edward Lazenby here, this could have been a worse tragedy." He rose and straightened imaginary wrinkles from his trouser legs. "Anyway, please accept our heartfelt condolences, and my humblest apologies."

She nodded and reached out and patted

his hand.

"Who'll be conducting the memorial service?" Ed asked.

"I will," Vickers replied. "And, fear not, it will be brief."

And, it was. Ed was surprised, nay, dumbfounded. Vickers gave a moving memorial tribute to Beatrice Terwilliger, even admitting that he didn't know her will, but saying, "That doesn't really matter. Even though our contact with each other might be minimal, we are still family, and the loss of one diminishes us all." Thankfully, he made no mention of *how* Beatrice died, or the role Ed and Ernie had played in correcting that misunderstanding. He kept it brief, thanked everyone for coming, and stepped from behind the pulpit to again express his condolences to Zelda, and then walking out of the church. Ed thought the man would have made a pretty good preacher—not that he had all that much experience with preachers—but, he was a good speaker.

It had been an amazing morning, a miraculous morning, filled with surprises. First, Vickers exhibiting human traits, instead of his usual pompous, aloof bureaucratic self, and then Zelda—there was the greatest miracle of all—from not insisting to Vickers that she was just 'Zelda,' when he addressed her as Ms. Terwilliger, to the physical transformation from Goth/punk rocker to an attractive, put-together young lady. She'd just lost her aunt and her brother, but she was taking it all well.

Oh, and Petunia had, as Rose had promised, remained quiet and well-behaved for the entire memorial service.

After the service, of course, several people made their way to the front before Ed could leave, ostensibly to personally express their condolences, but mainly to congratulate him on solving yet another mystery. Trapped, he had no choice but to shake their hands and acknowledge their praise with a modest nod and smile.

The day of bright, shining miracles had, for Ed, suddenly turned gloomy. Zelda saved him finally by pleading a headache and Rose followed up by suggesting that the six of them—she insisted on including Petunia in any activity—adjourn to her house; Violet frowned at this, since the lease was in *her* name, but said nothing—for tea.

As they strolled down Palm toward Maple for the approximate half-block walk, Ed assessed the day. He didn't like being the center of attention, but Zelda, Rose . . . and even Violet to a degree . . . had come to his rescue. The sky was blue, and the temperature was mild for early June. The wind was blowing, not too hard, just a soft caress on his face. He was with friends.

Suddenly, he didn't feel so gloomy after all.

Charles Ray

Thirty-two

On Monday morning, Ed's phone rang, just as he was entering his house, returning from having breakfast with Ernie, Violet and Rose at the community center. It was Detective Carl Janzen. He informed Ed that he wanted to talk to him *and* Ernie, *together*, and that he would be at Ed's house at 10:00 on the button. Ed didn't like the way he'd emphasized certain words, nor was he particularly comfortable with the ominous tone of the cop's voice, but he called Ernie and informed him anyway.

At 9:45, the two of them were sitting in Ed's living room staring at two mugs of untouched, and now cold, coffee.

"What do you think he wants to talk about?" Ernie asked.

"Darn if I know," Ed said. "But, he didn't

sound like it would be anything good."

A flash that lit up the gloom of the living room even though the curtains were closed, followed closely by a series of explosive booms, caused both of them to nearly jump off the sofa.

"Shit," Ernie said. "That was close."

"Sure was. It's a little early in the year for thunderstorms. They usually wait until July."

The next 'flash,' and Ed could have sworn he heard a 'zizzle' sound, and immediate clap of thunder that sounded like an artillery barrage, was closer and even louder than the first, but, expecting it, they didn't flinch.

"It's climate change," Ernie said. "The weather patterns have all gone to shit."

"Maybe."

"Either that, or an omen. I'll bet this is a sign of Carl's mood. He's coming to ream us out about sticking our noses in police business again."

As much as Ed hated to admit it, and buy into Ernie's superstitions, there *was* a chance that lambasting them was precisely what Janzen had in mind. His tone of voice certainly leaned in that direction. He walked to the window beside the front door and flipped the curtain back. Outside, the sky was dark and threatening. A flash of nearby lightning caused him to back away slightly, and when the crash of thunder followed, he flinched involuntarily. Despite the hour, it was as dark outside as the hours of twilight.

Suddenly, pellets of rain slammed against the window, sounding like pebbles. The rain, angled sidewise by the wind, started coming in a staccato torrent, sounding like popcorn at the height of popping, or small caliber bullets smacking against a brick wall. He didn't really believe in omens, but if he did, this wouldn't be a good one.

He let the curtain fall back into place and turned to face his friend.

"It's coming down hard out there. Maybe Carl won't come."

Ernie looked at his watch, a gold-colored fake Rolex that his colleagues had presented to him when he retired.

"It's 9:55," he said. "Maybe you're right, but that only postpones our whipping."

As if Mother Nature agreed with him, a series of lightning flashes sizzled through the sky at the same time, accompanied by a barrage of thunder that caused the walls to vibrate. Ed could feel the hairs on his arms tingling. He shook himself and returned to the sofa. He picked up his cup and took a long swig of the now-cold coffee.

"Yew, this is terrible. I'm gonna make a fresh pot."

Ernie picked up his cup, took a sip, grimaced, and spit the cold, brown liquid back into the cup. "Please do," he said.

Ed took both cups into the kitchen. After pouring the cold coffee, from the cups and the coffee maker, down the drain, he rinsed everything and set a fresh batch brewing. He stood there, watching the coffee burble and slurp as a brown stream fell from the hole in the bottom of the filter holder, slowly pooling and rising in the glass pot below, and listening to the undiminishing sound of thunder echoing throughout the house. The lightning was flickering like the strobe lights of a disco ball, blasting through the open curtains over the kitchen windows and causing his vision to flicker and blur. A couple of times the lights in the house flickered. He hoped PEPCO, the electrical utility serving the area, had crews standing by. A community of elderly people doesn't do too well with power outages. Worse, he thought, was that if the electricity went out, which it occasionally did during bad weather, the cable, providing TV, telephone, and Internet, would go out as well, or worse, the power would stay on, and the cable would go out. Oh, the stink that would cause, he thought. All of the goodwill Vickers had gained from the way he handled the memorial service would be washed away in the torrent of complaints. He chuckled at the thought. He didn't dislike the man, just what he stood for, bureaucratic self-serving indifference. Actually, he thought, maybe it should just be bureaucratic self-serving, that way it would be BS, which is what it is. He smiled at his wit.

He was still smiling when he returned to

the living room with two fresh mugs of coffee. He handed one to Ernie, and took a long swallow from his own.

"What you smiling about?" Ernie asked after taking a sip and smacking his lips. "The wind with this thunderstorm's gonna mess up our shrubbery, and might just break down a few tree limbs 'n break windows, and Carl's comin' to ream us out for stickin' our noses in police business . . . what you got to smile about."

Ed told him what he'd thought about what any storm damage might do to Vickers' reputation, which brought a smile to his swarthy face.

"Well," he said. "I guess every cloud *does* have a silver lining."

The doorbell rang. They both looked at each other, and then at their watches. It was 10:15. The doorbell rang again, and again.

Ed rose and went to the door. He looked through the peephole. He could see a tall, hunched figure being pelted by the unrelenting rain. He opened the door.

Carl Janzen, his hair plastered to his head, his blue suit soaked and clinging to his muscular frame, pushed past Ed and strode into the living room, leaving a trail of water behind him.

"What took you so long? It's comin' down in buckets out there," Janzen growled.

"You're late," Ed said.

The detective whirled around and glared

at Ed, the effect somewhat muted, though, because of his soaked and disheveled appearance. "Late! You kiddin' me? You see that shit outside? I'm lucky I made it and not get sideswiped by some idiot who don't have a clue how to drive in bad weather."

"Why didn't you just postpone your trip?"

Janzen wiped water from his face. He shook, tossing droplets of water aside like a shaggy dog after a bath. "The storm started after I'd already left the precinct, so I figured, what the hell, might as well keep going. I nearly got run off the road three times between Rockville and here." He sniffed the air. "Say, can I get a cup of that coffee?"

"Sure," Ed said. "If you'll wait a minute, I'll get a drop cloth and find you a place to sit. You want to take your jacket off? I can hang it over the back of a chair in the kitchen to dry."

Janzen took his jacket off, adjusted the service weapon in the holster high on his left hip, and handed the sodden jacket to Ed.

Ed went to the kitchen, carefully arranged the jacket over the back of a chair and placed it near the door. He went to the pantry, where he found the heating fan he used to warm the air on chilly evenings when he wanted to sit on his patio, plugged it in and set it on the floor four feet from the chair. He set it to oscillate and on medium heat, which he estimated would dry the coat in ten minutes or so, at least enough for Janzen to wear it comfortably. He then filled a large ceramic mug with coffee and went back to the living room.

Ernie, sitting, and the big detective, standing, were looking at each other, saying nothing, when Ed walked in and handed Janzen the mug of coffee. Janzen blew on it and then took a long swallow. Ed went into his second bedroom, which he used as a storage space and office. Folded in the corner near the closet was the canvas drop cloth he'd used when he painted the kitchen walls. He took it back to the living room and spread it over one of the chairs facing the sofa, and motioned Janzen to sit.

For a long time the three of them sat, silently sipping their coffee and not looking at each other over the rims of their cups.

Finally, Ed could take the suspense no longer. "Look," he said. "I know we promised that we wouldn't stick our noses in police business anymore, but this was a special situation."

Janzen leaned forward to put his cup on the coffee table. The drop cloth made snapping sounds as his weight shifted. He sat back and glared fiercely at them for thirty seconds, his lips twitching. Then, he leaned forward, slapping his upper thighs and began laughing.

"What's so funny?" Ernie asked.

"Did I tell a joke?" asked Ed.

Janzen laughed harder. He laughed until

tears streamed from his eyes, and then he laughed some more. Ed and Ernie sat, perplexed and not a small bit angry. Finally, Janzen stopped laughed. He hiccupped. He wiped his eyes, and looked at them with a big lopsided grin on his face.

"You should see the looks on your faces," he said. "Damn if it wasn't worth driving out here in that storm and nearly getting drowned just to see it."

"Do you mind telling us what you're talking about," Ed said.

"You guys thought I was coming here to chew you out, right?"

They nodded. "Of course," Ed said. "Why else would you be coming . . . oh, I forgot, you have our statements for us to sign?"

"Well, no in fact, I don't. They didn't get them transcribed as quickly as I thought. Besides, if I'd brought paperwork, it would've just gotten soaked."

"So, what did you come for?" Ernie asked. "The coffee?"

Janzen took a sip and smiled. "Well, that would have been worth it. This is so much better than that crap they have at the precinct, and I hate having to plunk down four bucks at Starbucks." He took another sip, his eyes twinkling at them over the cup rim.

Ed stamped his foot. "Would you please stop playing with us?"

Janzen put the cup down and eased back,

again causing the drop cloth to make an annoying cracking and popping sound.

"Okay," he said. "I came to fill you in on what went down after we left.

Ed and Ernie visibly relaxed. Their frowns of worry were replaced by looks of anticipation.

"First, I don't know what you did to make Terwilliger talk . . . and, please don't tell me . . . but, when we got him in an interrogation room, he started spilling his guts before we could even take the cuffs off. I mean, he told us everything."

"About how and why he killed his aunt?"

"Yeah, that and much, much more. He dropped a dime on Jerome 'Jerry' Stark and his gang, too. It seems that Stark's had his hand in a lot of the nasty stuff going on in this part of Montgomery County for a while now; loan sharking, prostitution, stolen cars, extortion, drug trafficking, you name it. He'd been using Terwilliger and his garage to chop stolen cars so they could sell the part. He was also the kid's main coke supplier. Unfortunately, Terwilliger sucked more stuff up his nose than his work in the garage could cover, and Stark was pressing him for payment. When he told them about his wealthy old aunt, they convinced him to drug her with the PCP and steal from her. When they found out he'd accidentally given her too much and killed her . . . the asshole called them on his mobile . . . they told him to steal the will so the original will would be in effect, and he could share his half of her estate with them, and his debts would be cleared.

He paused and took another sip of coffee.

"Needless to say, we were busy Saturday and much of yesterday rounding up Stark and his goons. When we confronted them with the evidence of Terwilliger's phone call to Stark's number on May 26, Stark started weakening, but when we questioned his man, Turk, the one who gave the kid the drugs, he folded immediately and ratted his boss out; told us the drugs were Stark's idea."

"Oh my," Ed said. "This was even more involved than I thought."

"You bet your ass it was," Janzen said. "And, if it hadn't been for you two poking sticks into the hornet's nest, they would've gotten away with it. You not only solved Beatrice Terwilliger's murder, you were instrumental in putting away one of the biggest scumbags in the county. So, you see, I didn't come here to fuss at you. I'm here to say thanks. You guys did good, real good."

"So, you're not gonna tell us not to stick out noses into police business?" Ernie asked.

"No way in hell. I'm still required to warn you not to interfere with official police business. You're just amateurs, and you could get hurt." He took another sip of coffee. "So, since I know you two old farts are gonna ignore me, I guess all I can say is, please be careful."

"Always," Ed said.

"For sure," Ernie added.

"Good, now can I have another cup of this fine coffee?"

As Ed poured the coffee, he noticed that he couldn't hear the sound of thunder, nor did he see the flash of lightning through the slit where the curtains didn't quite meet. He put the pot down and walked to the window. He drew the curtains aside. The sky had cleared; it was now gunmetal silver with just a wispy daubing of clouds. The thunderstorm had passed.

Charles Ray

Other books by this author:

Ed Lazenby mysteries
Butterfly Effect
Coriolis Effect
The Cat in the Hatbox
Al Pennyback mysteries
Color Me Dead
Memorial to the Dead
Deadline
Dead, White, and Blue
A Good Day to Die
The Day the Music Died
Die, Sinner
Deadly Intentions
Death by Design
Till Death Do Us Part
Deadly Dose
Dead Man's Cove
Dead Men Don't Answer
Deadly Paradise
Kiss of Death
Death in White Satin
Death and Taxis
Deadbeat
A Deadly Wind Blows
Death Wish
Deadly Vendetta
A Time to Kill, A Time to Die
Dead Ringer
Death of Innocence
Dead Reckoning

The Buffalo Soldier series

Buffalo Soldier: Trial by Fire

Buffalo Soldier: Homecoming

Buffalo Soldier: Incident at Cactus Junction

Buffalo Soldier: Peacekeepers

Buffalo Soldier: Renegade

Buffalo Soldier: Escort Duty

Buffalo Soldier: Battle at Dead Man's Gulch

Buffalo Soldier: Yosemite

Buffalo Soldier: Comanchero

Buffalo Soldier: Range War

Buffalo Soldier: Mob Justice

Buffalo Soldier: Chasing Ghosts

Buffalo Soldier: The Piano

Other fiction

Angel on His Shoulder

She's No Angel

Child of the Flame

Pip's Revenge

Wallace in Underland

Further Adventures of Wallace in Underland

Dead Letter and Other Tales

The White Dragons

The Dragon's Lair

Dragon Slayer

The Last Gunfighters

The Culling

Frontier Justice: Bass Reeves, Deputy U.S. Marshal

Angel on His Shoulder-Revised Edition

Battle at the Galactic Junkyard

Mountain Man

Devil's Lake

Nonfiction

*Things I Learned from My Grandmother About
Leadership and Life*

*Taking Charge: Effective Leadership for the
Twenty-first Century*

Grab the Brass Ring

*African Places: A Photographic Journey
Through Zimbabwe and southern Africa*

A Portrait of Africa

There's Always a Plan B

*In the Line of Fire: American Diplomats in
the Trenches*

Advice for the Insecure Writer

Looking at Life Through My Lens

Children's books

The Yak and the Yeti

Samantha and the Bully

Molly Learns to Share

Where is Teddy?

Catie and Mister Hop-Hop

Charles Ray

About the Author

Charles Ray has been writing fiction since his teens. He won a Sunday school magazine writing contest when he was thirteen, and having his byline on a short story published in a national publication forever hooked him on writing. During his time in the army (1962-1982) he often moonlighted as a newspaper or magazine journalist, and was the editorial cartoonist for the Spring Lake (NC) News, a weekly newspaper, during the 1970s. In addition to his writing, he was an artist/cartoonist and photographer for a number of publications, including Ebony, Eagle and Swan, and Essence, and had a monthly cartoon feature and did several covers for Buffalo, a now-defunct magazine that was dedicated to showcasing the contributions of African-Americans to the country's military history.

After retiring from the army, he joined the U.S. Foreign Service, and served as a diplomat in posts in Asia and Africa until his retirement in 2012. He has worked and traveled throughout the world (Antarctica is the only continent he hasn't visited), and now, as a full time writer, continues to globetrot looking for interesting things to write about, draw, or take pictures of.

A native of Texas, he now calls Maryland

home. For more on his writing and other projects, check one of the following Web sites:

http://charlesaray.blogspot.com
http://charlieray45.wordpress.com
http://www.twitter.com/charlieray45
http://www.facebook.com/charlieray45
http://www.flickr.com/photos/charlesray45/
http://www.viewbug.com/member/charlesray